# SOUL CATCHER

Katia
Spiegelman

# SOUL CATCHER

a novel

Marion Boyars
New York · London

Published in Great Britain and the United States in 1990 by
Marion Boyars Publishers
26 East 33rd Street, New York, NY 10016
24 Lacy Road, London SW15 1NL

Distributed in the United States and Canada by
Rizzoli International Publications Inc, New York

Distributed in Australia by
Wild & Woolley Pty Ltd, Glebe, NSW

© Katia Spiegelman 1990

All rights reserved.

No part of this publication may be reproduced, stored in a retrieval system or transmitted in any form or by any means, electronic, mechanical, photocopying, recording or otherwise except brief extracts for the purposes of review, without prior permission of the publishers.

Any paperback edition of this book whether published simultaneously with, or subsequent to, the casebound edition is sold subject to condition that it shall not by way of trade, be lent, resold, hired out or otherwise disposed of without the publishers' consent, in any form of binding or cover other than that in which it was published.

British Library Cataloguing in Publication Data
Spiegelman, Katia
  Soul Catcher.
  I. Title
  813.54 [F]

Library of Congress Cataloging in Publication Data
Spiegelman, Katia, 1959–
  Soul Catcher : a novel / Katia Spiegelman.
  I. Title.
PS3569.P4794S68   1990
813'.54 – dc20                90–32608

ISBN 0–7145–2908–7 Cloth

Typeset in 11/13pt by
Ann Buchan (Typesetters), Shepperton, Middx.
Printed in Great Britain by
Billing & Sons Ltd, Worcester

# For my parents: Joel, Gail & Russell

# ACKNOWLEDGEMENTS

Thanks to all the friends who read and responded to this story. Special appreciation goes to Margaret Kiley, who convinced me to send it into the world; and to Phyllis and Ebe Kronhausen, who introduced the book to my publisher, Marion Boyars.

I am also indebted to my entire family. Thanks to my grandmother Frances Voelker who, with my late grandfather Edward, put me through graduate school, during which time I first drafted this novel.

And thanks to Matt Cahill for listening to pages read aloud from subsequent drafts, and helping with fine-tuning.

# PART ONE

# ONE

I don't know why they called it Grove. The campus was surrounded by roads and telephone poles. An invisible fence kept us in, encapsulated in a world formed by specific standards and rules. I stumbled over boundaries right away: fell in love with the *wrong* boy, made the *wrong* friend. Patrick and Gwen taught me how to resist feeling entrapped by Grove. It was supposed to be a special school — progressive — but it was just another loony bin. We were delinquents, addicts, mental cases, orphans and kids from broken homes. We ranged from nuts to normal. Everyone had a peculiar story, a schism in their past through which they'd fallen into Grove. Except me. I didn't know why I was sent there, not at first.

It was 1973. Meeting Gwen was the beginning. We met on my second day at school; I was one day ahead of her in the Great Grove Indoctrination, but she knew so much more.

She was due at any moment and I had to get ready fast. I rushed into our room directly after classes, and dropped my books on my neatly made bed. Gwen's, across the room, was still a naked mattress. I didn't want her to find me in the blue woollen jumper that fit Grove's dress code, but not me. My real clothes were faded denims with ripped knees, a black tee-shirt with a big yellow sun on the front, and my good old beat-up red ProKeds. The jumper had a long zipper in the back — the kind you can never reach — and just when I got it halfway down, the nasty metal teeth took a bite of my bushy hair. I only brushed it once a day, in the morning; the rest of the time it went wild. Now it was snagged in the zipper. I arched back and just managed to reach the knot of metal and hair.

'Practicing your yoga?'

I twisted round and saw a blond girl with two huge suitcases standing in the doorway.

'My hair's caught!'

She walked over, gently freed my hair and pulled the zipper down.

'There,' she said, and looked around the room: at the unclaimed bed in the corner, with its old stained mattress and pile of starched white sheets at the foot; at the small beaten dresser next to it; at the warped wooden floor; at the cream-colored cinderblock walls.

'I guess that's my bed,' she said. 'I guess you're my roommate.'

Gwen was wiry and cute. Her hair was silky straight and defined by a perfect side part. A sky-blue tee-shirt clung to her small breasts.

'It's not so bad, I guess.' Her voice strained as she dragged her suitcases across the room, clomping in platform shoes. 'I've been in worse. Posters and throw rugs will help, maybe a little incense.'

I am an only child and wasn't used to undressing in front of others. So I sat on my bed in the blue jumper, zipper fanned open across my back, and told her about what she'd missed on the first day of school.

'We're only allowed off campus on Saturday afternoons,' I said. 'We can go to the mall down the road and get what we need. Usually after classes you get half an hour to change for activities. Activities sign-up isn't until tomorrow, so this afternoon is free.'

'Activities?'

I shrugged.

'I don't believe in schedules and rules,' she said, and snapped open the latches of the biggest suitcase. She was so neat. Clothes came out of her suitcase in perfect piles and went into her dresser in perfect piles. She made her bed with hospital corners, then covered it with a red-striped Indian bedspread, making sure the edge fell to an inch above the floor all around. She carefully arranged her things on her dresser: comb, nail file, jewelry box, lava lamp, roach clip. I mentioned that, according to school rules, roach clips were strictly forbidden, not that I cared.

'Why?'

'Because if they catch you doing anything wrong —'

'What's wrong about a roach clip? *Jesus.*' She rolled her eyes.

'No drugs, no drinking, no sex. No drug paraphernalia.'

'Sure, sure, sure.'

'No, really. They'll expel you for that. Patrick told me all about it. He's my boyfriend.'

She eyed me. 'Boyfriend?'

'Yup.'

'How long have you been here?'

'Just since yesterday.'

'Fast worker.' She winked.

'Patrick was here last year and he told me all about it. They'll expel you for any little rule you break.'

'Let them. I don't want to be here anyway.'

'But if they *know* you want to leave, they won't expel you, they'll room you or anything but let you go. It's complicated. Basically what it comes down to is they won't let you have what you want.'

'Yeah, just like every-fuckin-where else.'

'If you do want to be here and they expel you, then you have to talk your way back in. Patrick said that means telling them what they want to hear.'

'Who's *them?*'

'I'm not sure. So far I think it's just Silvera. He's the principal.'

'Yeah, right.'

But from what I had heard, you did follow the rules or get into big trouble.

After a while, Gwen began to tell me about herself. Her parents had been divorced since she was a baby. She said she'd had so many stepmothers she couldn't even count them, and that her father was engaged again. Her mother was an alcoholic who managed to hold down a job as a secretary, but had let everything else fall into disarray. Gwen alone had kept their home in New Jersey clean. But no repairs had been made on the house since her father had left fourteen years ago, and it was falling apart. Gwen said, 'It's hopeless, you know?' with a matter-of-factness that saddened me. She seemed so tough and cool. She swore she would never go back home, ever.

'So what about you? Parents divorced?'

The question startled me. 'No. Mom and Dad are pretty solid.'

'So why'd they send you here?'

'I don't know, they just did.'

'You shitting me?'

'No.'

'There's something they're not telling you.'

'Like what?'

'I don't know, but take it from me, when the closet door's locked there's always a skeleton rattling inside.'

'Actually,' I lied, 'I wanted to go away. Nothing ever happened. I got sick of it, you know?'

'Do I know! But what I got sick of was something was always happening. Every time my mother heard about my father getting married again, she'd go on a binge. Drunk for weeks. It was *terrible*.'

'How would she find out? Do they speak?'

'Nah. I guess she hears about it from me. I know it would be better if I kept my mouth shut, but you know how it is.

One thing leads to another.' She curled her toes until the joints cracked.

'I'm glad my parents aren't divorced,' I said.

'It's not as bad as it sounds. They lose their united front routine. You get to do more what you want. That's sort of why I'm here. I mean, I got to doing some things my therapist thought were putting me on the wrong road.' She grinned. 'Anyway, it really wasn't so bad. I was selling a little dope on the side, made some bucks. So they took it all and sent me here. Raw deal. Parents are all crooks. I know as a fact my last step-mom got high all the time. She turned me on once.'

'Wow.'

'Do you smoke?'

'No.'

'Never?'

'I never liked cigarettes.'

'*Dope.*'

'Oh! Yeah, sometimes.' Another lie. The truth was, I had never smoked marijuana.

She opened an enamel box on her dresser and pulled out a fat white joint. She ran it under her nose, then twirled it between her thumb and forefinger.

'Maybe later I'll get you off.'

I shrugged. 'Sure, maybe.'

She threw her legs over the side of her bed. 'Hey, I'll show you something else if you promise to keep this between us.' She leaned over and pulled a suitcase out from under the bed. She popped open the latches and lifted the top. From under neatly folded piles of sweaters, she extracted a glossy magazine. Before I could see what it was, she tossed it over to me. I just barely caught it. It was a copy of *Playgirl*, picturing a hairy, musclebound man in a pair of black fishnet underpants. His hands rested on his hips and he smiled coyly at the reading public. I dropped it on the floor, where the pages fanned apart and fell open to an article titled 'Woman, Know Yourself: The Male Animal in All of Us.'

Gwen laughed. 'Oops.' She jumped up and retrieved the magazine. 'Guess you're not quite ready for this.'

'That's okay,' I said. 'It's just not my thing.'

She smirked. 'Girls don't have *things*. Or maybe you haven't discovered that yet.' She hid the magazine beneath the sweaters and slid the suitcase back under the bed. 'Any time you want to read it, you know where it is.'

She had a black lace negligée hidden in a rainboot at the back of the closet, a pack of rolling papers in the pocket of a pair of old jeans which she kept permanently at the bottom of her laundry hamper, and a can of forbidden hairspray concealed in a deodorant wrapper right on the bathroom shelf. She told me that no one else in the whole world knew about any of these things, and made me swear on my life that I would never breathe a word of it to anyone, even Patrick. I promised. But as the first week of school progressed, I realized she was putting various other girls in the dorm through the same paces. It was her way of creating a network of trust: secrets bound people to her. I didn't understand her, and thought she was *different*. But she wasn't that different in content, just in style. Other people had secrets, too.

# TWO

The dorms were two stone buildings set nearly at a right angle, connected by an archway. Small windows were like portholes looking out onto the green, wild outdoors. Rumor had it that the school was originally built as a music conservatory. Supposedly there were to have been five dorm buildings in all, and they were to have formed a circle. There was something monastic about the cold stone dorms, an aloofness that could make you lonely just by being in them. But if you looked at the buildings for what they were once supposed to have been — a place where young, serious musicians would come to isolate themselves against the impure world and focus on music — then for a moment a special aura could envelop the place. When I first heard the story, I stood in front of Upper Girls and, staring at the row of mirrory windows, conjured up a feeling of brilliance and purity and art. It was a thrilling moment, and it faded too fast. Gwen claimed she could sustain that feeling for days at a time. She had a fantasy that we were the protégés.

'But we're not musicians,' I said.

She shook her head and her silky hair swayed. 'It doesn't matter. We just haven't found our exact tunes.'

Patrick didn't believe in any of it. He didn't believe the

story, and he didn't trust our faith in it. 'They don't even teach music here,' he said. 'Anyone who wants to learn music wouldn't come to this school.'

It was true. Life at Grove was strict and generally uninspiring. We were woken up at seven o'clock, had breakfast at eight. In the interim we showered (maybe), put on our *nice* clothes for the school day and thoroughly cleaned our rooms. This meant that every single morning we dusted, swept and straightened up. Then we hurried down the hill to lower campus to be outside the dining room when, rain or shine, the door was opened at precisely eight o'clock. We stood behind our chairs with studied obedience until given the magic word to sit.

A typical breakfast was greasy scrambled eggs, soggy Wonder Bread toast, metallic tasting orange drink, and weak coffee drunk from glasses like Russians drink their tea. While we ate, the dorm parents checked the rooms. Dorm parents were teachers who lived in the dorms with us, three to a floor. It was usually just after breakfast was served that the dorm parents came down to the dining room and searched for their prey: he or she whose bedspread touched the floor, or whose garbage can contained a tissue, or on whose floor there had been found a piece of straw from the broom. These students were sent back up to the dorm to clean their rooms again. They would wait in the dorm until the dorm parents had finished breakfast, sat through the first faculty meeting of the day and rushed back up the hill to reinspect the rooms. Everyone from the dorms would then hurry down to the main campus and classes would begin. The only good thing about this early morning routine was that the students who didn't get sent up had extra time in the Smoking Circle. This was one of the few areas designated for smoking cigarettes. There were a few sawed-off tree stumps and a big log to sit on, and lots of grassy spaces in which to stand. Now, of course, there would be No Smoking signs all around. But back then, cigarettes were cool, not deadly. And drugs, well, they were good clean fun. It was a looser, crazier time than now. Barriers had broken down in the sixties, and we were the first generation of kids to cross over into the post-revolutionary rubble, to experiment in the new society, to play freely, to fly. Which is why so many of the kids at Grove had come to be there, in its relatively strict environment: they had flown too close to the sun.

Classes went until two-thirty, with a mid-morning break at twenty past ten and lunch at noon. After classes you changed into jeans, had activities, changed back into nice clothes and went down to dinner. After dinner you had precisely twenty minutes to change back into jeans and be down at the school building for two hours of study hall. And then, between nine-fifteen and ten o'clock, it was bliss. Teachers were holed in the dorms. Everything was over. Darkness provided a semblance of privacy and the fence in front of Lower Boys filled up with couples hugging and kissing and whispering until exactly nine-fifty-nine-and-a-half.

Patrick kissed me for the first time sitting on that fence. Oh, how I loved him, from the very beginning! How I wanted that kiss and waited for it, hoped for and dreamed of it. I never came right out and announced my innocence, but he knew it anyway. He'd had girlfriends before, but he was patient with me. He took things very slowly and was gentle with me all along. For two weeks we went everywhere together, holding hands, kissing each other, but only on the cheek. Then, finally, came the big kiss, the first flame that burst from our original spark.

I met Patrick on the very first night of school. Everyone was packed into the basement dining room. The low, stucco ceiling gave it the feeling of a cave. And it was damp. One wall had four windows that let in a little light. The other walls were covered with murals: bright, primitive scenes in which children scampered up hills, or sledded down curvy paths, or stood in a circle holding hands like some kind of congress of brotherly love. Crazy Hal the dishwasher stood in the doorway leading to the steamy room that housed the ancient dishwashing contraption that left the glasses covered with a gritty film. He only had a few teeth and came from a mental ward somewhere. He never spoke.

After dinner, Gene Silvera stood up and paced until the room fell silent. He was the principal of Grove. I had already heard him referred to as *the fat man*. He was wearing a fluorescent orange tashika with a bold swirling African print. With his jet black hair, grizzly beard, deep brown eyes and olive skin, he reminded me of an angry bull. He moved back and forth, back and forth through the silence as if it were a stretch of earth he was wearing down, as if he were preparing soil or marking territory.

The man frightened me, Grove frightened me, being away from home frightened me. A tightness gripped my throat, a fledgling sob. I tried to force back the sound, but that only made it worse, and finally a miserable choking sound escaped into the silence.

Silvera spun around and looked straight at me. He just stared and stared with his blazing eyes locked into mine. He wouldn't let go. I was terrified, and in that instant my fear disappeared. Like an animal who had been sniffed out as prey, the concentration of my whole being shifted to the immediate moment.

'As long as you dwell on the past,' Silvera said slowly and deliberately, finally detaching his gaze from me and shifting it from face to face, 'as long as you dwell on the past, as long as you *live* in your past, you will not experience it *here,* and until you experience it *here* you will never be able to leave.'

His pacing accelerated, then he stopped short. One hand shot up to stroke his beard and the other went straight above him to grab one of the pipes that snaked around the ceiling. His sleeve fell to his shoulder, revealing his hairy overgrown armpit. There were giggles. Silvera smiled, igniting a haughty wave of laughter, which dissolved abruptly as his smile vanished.

'This is exactly where you have to be at all times,' he said.

There was a flutter of confusion. What did he mean? Was he saying we could never leave the dining room? His voice rose above the din and he said, 'You are here, right *here, now,* at this very instant in time, and that is where you better stay or baby, you will never, and I mean *never,* get out of here.'

That really pushed my button and the fear rushed back.

'But you know what?' he said. 'And I guarantee this: You will not want to leave.' Excited, he sped up. He let go of the pipe and crossed the room in long, quick strides that made his stomach bounce spasmodically. 'The minute you feel that you gotta get outta here, that you have to go, that if you don't, you'll bust right here — ' he punched his stomach with his fist ' — then I can tell you you've *never* been here at all. And what you really want is to escape yourself. Once you are *here,* right here, *now,* you will know *who* you are and *where* you are and you will know in your gut that it is the *only* place you can possibly be.' He paced, breathing heavily, nostrils flared.

I was staring into space, trying not to cry, when I had a feeling I was being watched. I thought it must be him (or as he probably thought of himself, Him), but when I raised my eyes to the massive orange man, I found him preoccupied by his thoughts, pacing, silent. Looking slowly to my right, I was met by a pair of smiling eyes. They belonged to a boy at the next table. He had a round, moonish face and a halo of curly orange hair. His skin was as white as rice paper. His eyes were a dark, soulful blue.

Silvera's voice boomed: 'You are a butterfly!'

Choking back a sudden rush of laughter, the tears I'd been suppressing welled up and dribbled down my cheeks. I thought I must have looked insane and turned to see if the boy had noticed. He was still looking at me, and he smiled. I could feel my face go red.

Silvera continued: 'Ugly! Selfish! But if you do it right, you have a chance to be beautiful and free.' He took between two fingers the medallion he wore around his neck and lifted it. 'I wear this butterfly to remind me why you are here, why I am here to help you. You're out of the cocoon but you're not beautiful yet, you're not free yet. You've got a lot of dealing to do before you'll know how to fly.'

There was a party in the dining room later that night. The tables were pushed against the walls, freeing a large space for dancing. Blue paper cloths were draped over the plain wooden tables, and colored streamers and balloons decorated the ceiling. There were two tables, one on either side of the room, with snacks and big bowls of fruit punch. Two boys with long stringy hair and bad acne appointed themselves deejays for the night. It was all Hendrix, Beck, Clapton, The Who, The Stones until three black girls bullied them into some soul. They said they were the 'Be Here Butterflies' and wanted to dance. The boys finally gave in and put on a record of Motown hits. The three girls lined up in front of the stereo. One was fat, another was tall and strong, and the third was tiny and slender. Their hair was identically braided in spirals starting from the center of their heads. When the music started, they lurched into their routine. They danced like clutzes, like talent show dropouts. Kids gathered around them and clapped and shouted. Soon almost everyone was dancing.

But not me; I was too nervous. I stood by the wall and tapped my foot. There was a bowl of salted mixed nuts next to me and I kept dipping my hand into it. I wasn't hungry, I just needed something to do. A strobe light beat against the room and I couldn't make out any familiar faces. Every flash was like an instant photo of frozen movement, one blinding snapshot after another.

'Nuts are really fattening, you know.' The boy from dinner had crept up next to me. He was wearing new jeans, blue Adidas and a blue and black plaid shirt with abalone snaps. He was skinnier than he had looked sitting down during dinner. He was very tall. Seated, his round face had made him look thicker, less striking.

'Hi,' he said.

I said, 'Hi.'

'But I wouldn't worry about it,' he said.
'What?'
'About nuts being fattening. I noticed you didn't eat much dinner.'

It was true, the greasy baked chicken and pasty mashed potatoes, obviously from packaged flakes, hadn't done much for my appetite. I'd only picked on some lettuce.

'It's my first day here.'
'I know, I was here last year. I'm a senior. You?'
'Sophomore.'
He nodded.
'I'm in Upper Girls.'
'All the girls are in Upper Girls. There are twice as many boys so they've got us split between two floors. I'm in Lower Boys. All the juniors and seniors are.' He smiled. 'Two boys to every girl. What's your name?'
'Kate.'
'I'm Patrick.'

We looked at each other in silence. My shoulders bunched from tension, and I tried to force them down.

'You okay?'
'I'm fine.'
'Listen, would you by any chance feel like dancing?'

A vision of myself jerking clumsily around in front of him popped into my mind. I froze. I couldn't say either yes or no.

Patrick said, 'Then how about taking a walk with me? It's kind of stuffy in here anyway. I bet you don't smoke.' He pushed forward a shoulder so I could see the red and white Marlboro box in his shirt pocket, and half smiled in a way I had always associated with hidden wisdom. He was a senior, after all. He must have been at least seventeen.

It was dark outside. The air felt damp and cool. We sat next to each other on the big log in the Smoking Circle, just sat there and glanced from each other to the sky to the ground. I had always dreamed about having a brother. I wondered if it could have been that fate had thrown us together because we looked so much alike — we both had red hair — and might have been siblings in another life. I imagined that this was what a relationship with a brother would be like, with messages and understandings passed in silence, just by looking at each other. Then again, I was glad he wasn't my brother, that he was an unrelated boy who had asked me 'out'. I decided I would count this as my first date.

'Can I ask you why you were crying at dinner?' he said.

'If you want to,' I said, staring at the sharp impression my knees made under my jeans.

He moved closer. He didn't touch me but I could feel warmth from his body. 'I remember my first night here,' he said.

I watched him as he spoke. His eyes were true blue and his face was clear and white, the only vivid thing in my vision. Only he was there, no trees, no buildings, no road, just Patrick's face, large and bright in front of me. I felt a mixture of relief and disappointment: relief that he was steering the conversation away from me, disappointment that I would have to keep my thoughts bottled up. Something about him made my heart say *yes, talk, release, pour out*.

'I was sixteen. . . How old are you?'

'Fifteen.'

'Well, I wasn't much older.' He glanced over at the school building where, in the basement, the party was still going on, at the rickety old tool shed next to the Smoking Circle, at the narrow path snaking from the dorms to the center of campus, as if trying to see them for the first time. His face was blank; he knew the place too intimately to take in just its surfaces. He said, 'I didn't want to be here either.'

'I guess I was so obvious, I — '

He shook his head. 'No, no, it's all right. You're allowed to feel that way if you want to. They try to make you feel home shouldn't matter because we're all here. None of us are home. They try to make us think that's how it's supposed to be, you know, that it's how it should be because that's how it is.'

'I don't know why I'm here,' I said abruptly, and it almost

sounded like an appeal. 'I mean, my parents, they just sent me here on the spur of the moment.'

Lines formed across Patrick's forehead, and he looked concerned and wise, as if he knew something I didn't, some news about my own predicament. I waited for him to say whatever was forming in his thoughts, but instead of speaking he just looked at me with a pained expression on his face. I felt responsible, as if I had somehow caused it.

'Where are you from?' I changed the subject.

'Right here on Long Island. Only child, nice house, parents divorced. I'm your typical suburban boy.'

'I don't think so. I mean, in my town the boys from broken families are different.'

Patrick seemed to enjoy this. 'How?'

'They hang out all the time in town, you know, drinking and getting high. They're really gross. I hate them.'

'It's good not to be like them?'

'Definitely.'

'Well, you're not like the girls from here.'

'But they seem nice.'

'*Nice.* That's not the word for them. You're nice, really nice. I could tell the first time I saw you.'

I felt like asking: If I'm so nice, why did my parents send me here?

Patrick slid off the log and bowed at the waist. He offered me his arm, and said, 'This must be our song.'

'I can't hear anything,' I said.

'Dance with me anyway.'

We let ourselves go, twisting and hopping and jumping and having more fun than I ever expected on my first night away from home. Patrick was easy to be with. He was gentle and direct and an even worse dancer than me.

Our first kiss!

Patrick sat on the fence and I stood in front of him. It was a chilly autumn night and we were bundled up in sweaters, hugging for extra warmth. He rubbed my back and looked into my eyes and didn't speak. Patrick had a sexy silence; he didn't say much, but when he looked at you and touched you, he just filled you right up. I could tell he was building up to a real kiss. But every time he moved his face a little closer, Scottie Hendrick — known as Major Loony — waddled by, singing: '1969! 1969! 1969!'

Scottie was disturbed but perfectly harmless. There were a few kids like that at Grove. Neil Benson, a.k.a. Ford Highway, was another: a skinny boy with a protruding chin bearing approximately nine whiskers, whose obsession was cars. Every time a car passed on the road during school break, he would leap high into the air and call out the year and make of the car. The Smoking Circle would break into applause. Then there was Harold O'Leary, who walked on the balls of his feet and carried a conservative brown briefcase. And Ned Jones, who lurked around campus and told gruesome stories about how he murdered people's pets. And Suzie Zuckerman, who was tall and heavy and wore a black wig lopsided on her head and heavy beige makeup that got all over her clothes. She made loud, abrupt statements that would surprise people, but when you thought about it she almost always made sense. Peter Prentice, another oddball, practiced Zen, swallowed raw grain like pills, and had this crazy fantasy of building a big geodesic dome for no apparent reason.

'Take a hike, Scottie!' Patrick said.

'Hike to where?'

'To the moon for all I care.'

'Hmm. I don't know if I could get there in time.'

'In time for what?' I asked, knowing what the answer would be.

'1969!'

We laughed.

'What happened in 1969?' Patrick asked.

Scottie beamed. He folded his short arms over his rotund stomach. 'Nixon was President and *To Tell The Truth* went off the air.'

'Good,' Patrick said. 'Now leave us alone.'

Another couple down the fence called him over and he waddled away, singing, 'To the moon, to the moon, to the moon!'

By now it was a quarter to ten. Patrick sighed, rolled his eyes and pulled me to him in a hug. He kissed my neck and from there moved with tiny gentle kisses over my cheek to my mouth. I puckered my lips to let him know it was all right. He pressed his lips hard against mine, flattening them, and I felt his tongue running over my teeth. After a minute he slipped his tongue right into my mouth. The sensation was not as strange as I had expected it would be; I knew how my own tongue felt and his felt about the same, just a little thicker and wetter. The real difference was having two tongues in my mouth at one time. They moved in a kind of dance. Kissing Patrick for the first time was like underwater ballet: grace without gravity: heaven: dreams. For me, this was the music of Grove: Patrick and our late-night, speechless harmony.

But dreams are only that, dreams. There was so much I didn't know. I didn't know that failures of self could qualify love, nor that love could contain them. I didn't know that Patrick had his own crazy dream, and that it would come to involve me. And I didn't know how soon.

# THREE

It was on a brilliant October afternoon that I first spiralled into Patrick's world. Red and yellow and orange leaves basked in the clearest of light. We went to our afternoon activities as usual. Gwen was with us. She and I were taking ceramics, and Patrick was taking basketball. The gym was next to the shed where ceramics was taught, across the street from central campus. Crossing that road was the one time, other than the weekly trip to the mall, that you were technically off campus without breaking any rules. We always got a thrill crossing it and would walk very slowly. Sometimes Patrick would walk back and forth until a car came. It was one of our jokes.

Once across, Gwen ran off to the whitewashed shed where Louise taught ceramics. Gwen liked to be on time. Louise, who was also the French teacher and dorm mother of Lower Girls, was engaged to marry Jimmy, the basketball coach, math teacher and dorm father of Upper Girls. Gwen had a theory that if she kept in 'ultra good standing' with Louise, positive (meaning lenient) dorm treatment by Jimmy would naturally follow. I think Gwen was also careful about spending too much time with Patrick and me. She would join us in the Smoking Circle or at the canteen and then abruptly leave. Most of my friendship with Gwen took place at night, after lights-out, in our closet. We would close the door, turn on the light, and sit facing each other on the floor in our nightgowns. We'd talk. Other than Patrick, a frequent topic was a boy named John. He was tall and skinny, wore raggedy jeans and had long stringy blond hair. He reminded me of the grubby kids from my hometown who would hang out, cursing at traffic and smoking pot. Of course, that was the kind of boy Gwen liked, the dangerous, risky type. But we couldn't tell if John liked her back. We would mull over these and other life issues until we were too tired, and then we'd turn off the light and slip into our beds.

Patrick's best friend, besides me, was Eddie. He was short and flabby and an obnoxious jerk, as far as I was concerned. He was always telling dirty jokes, which I ignored and Gwen rebutted with sharp remarks and rolling eyeballs. People laughed at him but it seemed that no one, other than Patrick maybe, really liked him. Eddie had requested Patrick as his roommate and Patrick hadn't objected, which was as good as announcing they were best friends. It bothered me that Eddie's bad taste might creep into their private conversations. I trusted Patrick, but he was a boy, and Eddie had a way of bringing out the worst in people. He would nudge and prod until a perfectly nice person would spit out something cruel. Like the time Ted, another Upper Girls dorm parent and generally acknowledged as one of the school's nice guys, refused to let Eddie sit at his table at dinner because he was a 'parasite'. But he was Patrick's friend, so I tried to tolerate him. He often sat with us at meals. He was also taking basketball, which meant I had to put up with him when I went with Patrick to the gym. Luckily, Eddie went down to the gym early every afternoon, and not with us. He had a mission, a stupid Eddie joke. Amy, the fat Be Here Butterfly, had signed up for basketball in her quest to lose weight, and Eddie appointed himself her tormentor. She would dribble the ball around the court for fifteen minutes before activities started, and Eddie would chase her. Sometimes she got so mad, she turned around and threw the ball right at his head. He spread a rumor that they had sex in the woods at night.

I went to the gym with Patrick and watched him take off his clothes. He had his basketball uniform on underneath. His long legs were covered with curly orange hair; hairy legs meant a boy was growing up. But his chest was smooth and his arms were slender and white, except for a recurring rash in the insides of his arms, which he told me came from sweating. He jogged over to Eddie and Amy and hopped and sidestepped and reached until he confused the ball away from them. He jumped up, and snapped the ball into the hoop.

I ran over to the ceramics shed and could tell by the silence that the period had already started. I crept in and sat down next to Gwen, hoping Louise wouldn't pay any attention. She was in the middle of demonstrating how to make a tall vase. But when she heard me, she looked up and her creation took a U-turn. The wheel slowed to a stop and she stared at me with squinty eyes. Her long brown hair hung in front of her narrow face. She wore black eyeliner and pink gloss on her lips.

'Hello Kate,' she said.

'Sorry.'

She shook her head as if she just didn't want to hear it. Personally, I think she understood; being in love herself, she knew how hard it could be to tear yourself away. For all the times I was late to ceramics, she never once reported me.

She tossed the ruined vase into one of the large bins by the wheel and scooped up a fresh lump of wet clay. She kicked and the wheel spun, and as the lump took form, growing narrow, hollow and tall, she doled out directions and advice. The trouble was that Louise didn't know much more about ceramics than we did. Ten minutes later, she had finished her demonstration and produced a rough, lopsided vase with such a tiny opening it probably would have strangled a flower.

'Now,' she said, as the wheel spun to a stop, 'let's see if you guys can make one like that.'

There were seven of us and only one wheel. Louise watched over each of us as we took her seat and tried to make a flower killer. One girl actually made a nice vase. A kid from Upper Boys made a bowl that he insisted was for low flower arrangements. Because it was getting late, Louise let it go.

I took my turn next and made the fastest vase in the east. It came up from the wheel like a time-lapse blade of grass, tall and straight and solid.

Louise looked at it and said, patiently, 'It's supposed to be hollow.'

'But it's *art!*'

She let that one go, too; in three minutes the period was supposed to end, and Jimmy would be waiting for her.

Troy was last. He was tall and beefy, with a head of long black hair that he never washed. He had this bad case of acne; he probably never washed his face, either. But he was the best friend of John, Gwen's fantasy Romeo, so we were both nice to him. Like mine, Troy's vase was tall and straight, but he managed to make his hollow. He poked two holes in the side with his finger.

Louise walked slowly around the wheel.

'It's a bong,' Troy said. He was kind of cute when he smiled. His face would glow and his brown eyes would turn up at the corners and look almost Oriental.

'I know what it is.' Louise pressed it back down into a blob of clay. 'Try again.' She looked at her watch. 'All right, the rest of you can leave, it's already late.'

That was a relief; we'd gone almost ten minutes overtime. I took off my clay-spattered apron and waited for Gwen. She was hovering around Troy, making noises about how unfair it was he had to stay after.

As we rushed to the gym, I couldn't resist telling her that I thought her publicity maneuvers were a little obvious. 'Troy's never going to talk to John about you, anyway.'

'How do you know?' she said. 'It couldn't hurt.'

'It's tacky.'

A few sweaty kids from basketball were standing in front of the gym, talking. I started to run, hoping Patrick hadn't given up waiting for me.

'V.J.!' Gwen called, running after me.

V.J. meant *value judgement*. Just the night before, in his after-dinner announcements, Silvera had declared that value judgements were bad and to be avoided. And so all day, people had been shouting V.J. at each other for the smallest things.

Eddie was inside the gym, sitting on the floor, tying his sneakers. His stomach bulged over his gym shorts. His short, heavy legs were pale and covered with dark fuzz. His wavy brown hair fell over his eyes and his thick lips pouted in concentration.

'Have you seen Patrick?' I asked him.

He looked up and shrugged. 'I dunno. I think he went to the woods to take a leak or something.'

'First you say you *don't* know, then you say you *do* know,' Gwen spat at Eddie. 'Hey man, do you even know where you are? I mean, like, what a shmo.'

'V.J., bitch!' Eddie said.

I left the lovebirds to go look for Patrick. I was just coming around the side of the gym to the small field that led to the woods, when I saw him. I thought he must have fallen down, because he was struggling up from the ground.

'Patrick!'

He tucked in his shirt and walked toward me with what seemed like a great effort. As he came closer, I noticed that his skin, which was usually pale, was so colorless it looked grey. His eyelids were heavy, and he was having trouble staying on his feet.

I put my arm around him and he leaned on me. 'What's wrong?'

'I'm fine.' His voice was slow and thick, syrupy.

'You're not feeling well? I wish we had time to sit down, but we'll be late for dinner.'

He leaned so much of his weight on me that I thought I'd collapse. I had no idea what was wrong with him. The flu, maybe, or stomach cramps from too much running. Whatever it was, he was in bad shape, and I was afraid we wouldn't make it across the road.

'I love you,' he hummed.

I felt a rush. He hadn't told me he loved me since the time we were standing in front of Girls Dorm, just before ten o'clock, when he whispered '*Te amo*' and kissed me. Since then, there had been moments I was afraid he'd stopped loving me. I wanted to tell him I loved him too. But before I could say it, his knees buckled and he was lying in the road. His eyes were glassy, staring at the sky.

'Are you going to be sick?' I said, leaning over him.

'I'm fine, just give me a minute.'

That's when I heard the sound of an engine coming toward us, and panicked. I said, 'Hurry up, a car's coming!' and tried to pull him up.

He wouldn't budge.

'Come on!'

Tamara the cook's gold Mustang skidded to a stop. She looked at us from the driver's seat, but didn't move or say anything. I could barely see her through the hazy windshield: a boxy dark-haired woman of thirty-five or so, with thick black eyebrows and a tiny nose. Then I noticed that there was someone with her. The door on the passenger side opened and Silvera lumbered out. His face was bright red as if he wanted to shout, or cry.

Patrick propped himself up on his elbows, and said, 'Oh *shit*.'

'Don't worry,' I said. 'You're sick.'

I thought Silvera was going to help us.

Patrick lurched onto his hands as if struggling with five hundred pounds. Silvera came toward us in even steps. His stomach wasn't bouncing; that meant he was sucking in his breath; and that meant he was really mad.

'He fell,' I said. 'He's sick.'

But Silvera wasn't in the mood to listen. We were *standing in* not *crossing* the road. We were technically off campus, breaking a rule.

'Get up!' he shouted.

Patrick got to his knees and was just beginning to stand, when Silvera's fist flew up and opened to a flat palm. His dark eyes settled on me. I was terrified and didn't know why. What had we done wrong, besides being in the road, that earned this much anger? The loud smack of his hand against my face startled me. Pain stung in my cheek. I clenched my teeth and did not cry; I knew now that I must never cry in front of this man again. Like the first night of school, when he pegged me as vulnerable. I stared at him and he stared back, shaking as if he were going to explode. Then, suddenly, he turned around and walked back to the car.

Patrick stumbled after him, screaming, 'Bastard! You goddamn fucking prick!'

The gold car drove slowly away. I stood there, stunned, and watched Patrick drop to his knees in the middle of the road. He flattened his palms on the asphalt and leaned forward. I realized he was crying when I saw tears falling straight down from his face to the ground, making a puddle.

All I could say was, 'What if another car comes?'

All he could say was, 'I'm so sorry, Kate. I'm so sorry.'

I still didn't know what we had done wrong, or why the man had slapped me, or what was wrong with Patrick. He didn't come down to dinner that night and he wasn't in study hall. All night long, with each minute he wasn't there, I became more confused. I was desperate to see him, to understand what was wrong with him. After study hall, Gwen took my books back to our room and I ran up to Lower Boys. Walter, a dorm parent, told me that Patrick was in Lower Girls 'visiting' with Silvera. *Visiting*. It was a transparently diplomatic choice of words. No one visited the fat man. You went to him to be challenged or accused or forgiven.

Silvera had a suite in Lower Girls, where the Little Kids lived. I hated going to him after he'd hit me, but I had no choice. Patrick was there. I couldn't wait any longer to see him. I took a deep breath and knocked. It was a minute before the door creaked open. Patrick was sitting in a bean bag chair on the floor. He peered at me as if I were a stranger; he said nothing, didn't even smile, just looked blankly at me, through me, beyond me. Then I heard Silvera's voice ask who it was, and Patrick muttered, 'Kate.'

'Come in!' Silvera said.

I pushed open the door and looked around inside. This was the first time I had seen the man's living room. He was slouched against a blue bean bag, directly opposite the door — like a frog king on a mushroom throne. Posters of seashores and sunsets decorated the walls. A plume of peacock feathers rose from a huge brass vase in the corner. He waved me in with the burning end of a filterless cigarette squeezed between two yellowed fingers.

I had never felt such coldness from Patrick as when I entered that room. He was in trouble, and I wanted to help him. But he was rejecting me; I felt it in the starkness of his silence. I hesitated, and almost turned around. Silvera told me to sit. I chose a red bean bag across from Patrick. Silence, cold and stark, froze me.

Finally Silvera spoke. 'Patrick has something to say to you.'

Patrick said nothing. He made a knot of his fingers and stared at it.

Silvera lit another cigarette. As he exhaled, he said, 'Patrick wants to apologize to you for this afternoon.'

When I heard that, anger ballooned in me and I nearly burst. How could he say that? He was the one who hit me! Not Patrick, *him*. Then a vivid memory of Patrick kneeling on the road, begging for my forgiveness, flashed like neon. Why?

Still, I said, 'No, not Patrick.' I strained against tears.

It was then, in my weakness, that Patrick found strength to look at me. He spoke solemnly, as if he knew the kind of emotion I was forcing back, as if he wanted to help me release it.

'Kate,' he said, very softly. 'I *am* sorry.'

Silvera leaned into his bean bag and watched us. He was like a voyeur of the soul, like an axe, a fierce eye intent on splitting love down the middle. I hated him.

'I'm sorry,' Patrick repeated in a shaking voice.

'But you didn't do anything,' I said. 'It was *him*.'

Patrick shook his head. 'It was me. It was my fault. He knew, that was all. He shouldn't have hit you. He wouldn't have if it hadn't been for me.'

'What are you talking about?'

Patrick slumped forward and dropped his face into his hands.

'Tell her,' Silvera said.

'I can't.'

'Tell her!'

I snapped, 'What if I don't want to know?'

Patrick's eyes were red, though he had stopped crying. I had never seen anyone so scared.

'Go ahead,' Silvera said.

'All right.' Patrick stared at his clasped hands, and said, 'I got caught — '

'No,' Silvera cut in. He leaned forward and shook his head quickly. 'No. Not *I got caught,* but *I am.* . . Go on. Say it.'

'I am not!' Patrick shouted in a loud voice that cracked. He was sobbing now. '*I am not!*' He sprang up from the bean bag and ran out of the room.

'Go find him and say goodbye,' Silvera said. 'He's leaving tonight.'

'I hate you.'

He smiled. 'No you don't,' he said, as he took a deep drag of his cigarette.

I tried to hit him with the meanest, most hateful look I could manage. But he stared back calmly, and my anger just boomeranged right back at me. It struck me suddenly that the man was too controlled not to be afraid. I didn't stop to think of what. I ran out, crying, and slammed the door as hard as I could.

Patrick was on his way from Boys Dorm to the main entrance of campus when I caught sight of him. His blue knapsack was slung over one shoulder. I ran after him down the hill, calling, 'Patrick! Wait!'

He kept walking. 'He expelled me!' he said.

'Why?' I kept running, trying to catch up.

I was surprised when he laughed. And hurt. 'Why not?'

Finally, I was next to him, trotting along, out of breath. 'What happened?' I pleaded. 'I don't understand what's going on.'

'I don't want to talk about it.'

'Please.'

'Kate, just leave me alone. I have to leave. There's nothing I can do about it.'

'Where are you going?'

'I don't know. Home, I guess.'

We were almost at the main entrance. A yellow taxi waited, its motor revving in the dark, empty road. I grabbed Patrick's arm. He pulled away and started to leave.

'Will you wait a minute?' I called.

'I have to go.'

'Patrick, *wait*.'

When he reached the road, he turned and looked at me, really saw me for the first time that night. His eyes were bright spots in a white face, undulating with emotion.

'I'll call,' he said.

He was really going; I was really losing him. As if the words could reel him back, I said, 'But I love you.'

He shook his head. 'That's not the point anymore, Kate.'

I watched the taxi become a yellow spot consumed by distance, then vanish. Nothing. Gone. I just stood there, staring, filled with a sensation of waiting. But for what? For Patrick to appear and come running toward me? For reality to reverse? To wake up?

What finally snapped me out of it was the sound of a sudden, piercing scream. It came from somewhere on the other side of campus and echoed way up into the blueblack sky. That scream brought me back to the moment, to me, Kate, standing alone in the dark on a deserted road. It wasn't like me to give myself to danger, or loneliness, or fear. Not until now. I ran up the hill and didn't stop until I was inside the dorm.

It was late. Gwen was waiting for me in the closet. She called me in and shut the door.

'Listen,' she said, 'I know all about it.'

'How?' I had told her about the slap, but how did she already know about Patrick leaving?

'Eddie told me,' she said. 'I made him.'

'Patrick's gone.'

She leaned over and hugged me, and I started to cry. 'Did you know about it?' she asked.

I pulled away and looked at her face. It was cool and serious. She waited for an answer.

'About what?'

She sighed. 'I don't believe it. You really didn't know? That's why the man slapped you, because he thought you knew. He must have figured you were letting it happen, maybe even helping him.'

'*What?*'

'Patrick,' she said. 'Heroin.'

The scream. Whose was it? That word *heroin* triggered the strangest thought: that somehow the scream had been mine.

# FOUR

I grew up in Westchester, in a big white Tudor house with blue window frames and a bright red door. Just my parents and me and our cat Betty. I figured Betty was one quarter Persian, because of her soft coat, one quarter tabby, because of the orange and brown stripes that circled her stomach like hula hoops, one quarter shorthair American, which some old alleycat member of her family had picked up on the street and which accounted for her long stretches of nondescript cat behavior, and one quarter Siamese, which would explain her mean streak. Betty was ten when I went away to Grove. In her younger days, and mine, she was condemned by my parents as a scourge. She would hang on screens until they ripped, and pee in the sink when there was a guest in the house. Dad said we should have the kitten terminated. Mom would just sit there and shake her head. They'd look at each other and laugh. That was their routine.

On the first homegoing weekend, I spent the bus ride into the city ignoring Gwen (who wanted to talk, as usual) for serious contemplation: I was worried about Patrick and Betty. I don't know why I was so upset about Betty — nothing had actually happened, except that I'd abandoned her and now would have to face the consequences. For all I knew, my parents had put her to sleep while I was away. My worries about Patrick were in the same vein. We had talked on the phone a few times since he was expelled from school. He was living with his mother on Long Island and working as a clean-up boy in a local deli. His mother wouldn't talk to him because he took drugs, he was a *bad boy,* not *her* son. Patrick claimed not to care. But he did, deep down. I could just tell. I had a theory that his mother felt responsible, maybe because of the divorce, or because she had been so poor afterwards and couldn't provide much. She felt guilty. She didn't expect her baby to grow up and get hooked on smack. No one does, especially not white, middle-class mothers whose sons are supposed to be doctors or lawyers or famous artists. The implication in her silence was that her thoughts were too terrible to put into words. Patrick felt guilty, too, about being home under the circumstances. It was as if by being home he was inflicting himself on her. I could hear in his voice that he was feeling bad about himself. He told me he had joined a methadone program. He said, 'It's great. No problem at all. I'm kicking it.' He sounded self-assured, but it wasn't that simple, because he was living in a hostile environment that was supposed to be home, with a silent woman who was supposed to be his mother. Did his mother want to terminate him, just like my parents wanted to terminate crazy old Betty when she was a pest?

It was dark out when the bus pulled into Port Authority in New York. Gwen and I hauled our suitcases into the terminal along with the rest of the kids. The bus ride into the city was provided by the school on the condition that the child was met at the station. Gwen and I were both being met by our dads.

'Shit!' Gwen hissed. She dropped her suitcase on the polished linoleum floor. 'He brought *her.*'

'Where?'

'Rabbit fur at high noon.'

Straight ahead of us, standing by a candy machine, was a slender woman in a hip-length, checkered, rabbit fur jacket.

She wore tailored slacks and very high heels. Her shaggy hair was hennaed and teased. I couldn't see her face: it was too busy being kissed by the balding, stumpy man whose hands were planted on the back of the fur jacket. A gold wedding band squeezed the man's bloated finger.

'Oh my God,' Gwen said. 'He went ahead and did it, he *married* her!' She turned around, frantic. 'Oh please Kate, *please* let me come home with you this weekend!'

'Come on,' I said.

She picked up her suitcase and glided around the corner, out of sight of her father. When I caught up with her, she was standing against a wall lighting a cigarette, cupping her hands around a tiny match flame. Her face lit up orange.

'Wait here,' I said. 'I'll go find my dad.'

I looked and looked, but couldn't see him anywhere. Finally, I stationed myself by the gate where our bus came in, thinking he'd look for me there. Meanwhile, Mr Perle (Gwen's dad) stood by that candy machine necking with his wife. It was disgusting. It made me nervous just to be near him, knowing he was such a sleazeball, and that he was waiting to take Gwen, and that she was just around the corner.

At last, Dad showed up. He came barrelling out of the throng in a blue suit, hauling the famous old briefcase he'd been using ever since law school. His salt-and-pepper hair was a bushy mess, but I thought he looked handsome. His red tie flapped over his shoulder as if from the wind he'd created by hurrying to reach me. It was an old joke of ours. Whenever he was late meeting me somewhere, he'd throw his tie over his shoulder and come running.

'My heels are on fire,' he said. He stooped to kiss my cheek. 'How's my girl?'

I hugged him with all my might.

'Mom can't wait to see you.' He picked up my suitcase.

'How's Betty?'

He smiled. 'She's fine.'

We were walking in the direction of the street exit, where

we could get a taxi to take us to Grand Central Station, when I heard the *clop clop* of footsteps running up behind us. In my excitement, I had completely forgotten about Gwen.

'Hey!' she called.

We turned around. There she was, dragging her suitcase, her eyes mean-narrow and her lips mad-tight.

'Fuckwad! What am I supposed to do?'

Dad looked at me with the blank expression that meant he was prepared to be surprised.

'That's Gwen,' I said, 'my roommate.'

She dropped her suitcase and sighed. 'You must be the old man,' she said.

Dad looked at me and I could see a glimmer of a smile.

We walked into the house and Betty flashed across the living room just like her old self. But when she tried to jump off the back of the couch, instead of clinging to the heavy fabric, she slid backwards.

'That's pathetic,' Gwen said.

'What's wrong with her?' I asked Dad.

'Mom's cooking dinner. Why don't you go say hello.'

I was no fool. He was ignoring me, which meant something was wrong. I picked Betty up and she patted my face with paws that felt like cotton balls. Gwen squeezed one of Betty's pads.

'This cat has been declawed!' she said. 'That's cruelty to animals, you know.' I pressed the pad of Betty's little white paw. No claws sprang out. *Nothing* sprang out. Gwen was right: they had removed her only defense against the world. Cruel world! I hugged poor Betty tight, and she tried to squirm away. I admit, she didn't seem too upset about the whole thing, but still, it was the principle. No one had asked me first; my parents had no right to maim my pet. I knew something was going to be wrong at home, I just knew it.

I marched into the kitchen, still holding Betty (by force). Dad had parked himself at the kitchen table. He was dipping his finger into a glass of scotch, tinkling the ice. Mom was at the stove, wearing a red canvas apron over her business suit, cooking. I was surprised. Mom and Dad had devoted themselves to their law practice: they were partners in their own firm in Manhattan. I grew up on spaghetti and hamburgers and baked chicken. Mom only cooked for special occasions, and this was just a regular Friday night.

She thrust a wooden spoon into an enormous pot of something, stirred, then turned around to cast one of her brilliant smiles upon me. The smile she claimed made Dad fall in love with her.

I wouldn't buy it.

'What did you do to Betty?'

'Hi, sweetheart. Welcome home! I'm making paella,' Mom said. Mrs Innocent.

'Betty, my cat, she has no *claws*, if you know what I mean.'

Dad tinkled his ice.

'Remember Betty?' I squeezed her pad so her fluffy, clawless paw fanned out.

'Betty's fine,' Mom said. 'It didn't hurt her. She was destroying the new chairs.'

Oh, the chairs. 'Since when is furniture more important than life?'

'It isn't, dear, we simply made a choice.'

Choices. Like sending me away to school. Random choices, as far as I could see.

'Ehem.' It was Gwen, standing behind me, clearing her throat.

'This is my roommate, Gwen,' I said. 'Dad said she could come.'

Mom flashed Dad a look, then said, 'Welcome! Make yourself at home.'

She did. Leave it to Gwen. She marched right over to the fridge, opened it, and said, 'No Tab?'

'Mix some juice with seltzer, dear,' Mom said. 'It's better for you.'

Gwen shrugged and closed the fridge. She sat with Dad at the table. I released Betty — who skidded out of the room

— and joined them. We all watched Mom stir and pour and organize. Her easy movements were like a thread, weaving us together, warming us, tugging back friendship. I wished I hadn't crashed in so meanly, despite Betty. I should have thought of Mom's feelings. Obviously this special dinner was for me.

As I watched her, I realized that Mom looked different somehow. Then it struck me that she had lost a lot of weight. She was never exactly fat, just a little chunky. But now she was thin. She looked tired. Her hair, twisted into the usual chignon, was laced with grey. Cooking, greying, declawing my cat. I had only been gone six weeks. Was Mom suddenly getting old?

She served a fabulous dinner of big bowls of paella over brown rice, French bread with sweet butter, and salad with olives and tomatoes and cukes and carrots and sprouts, my favorite. We even had dessert: chocolate éclairs from the bakery. The food was incredible! Conversation, though, was just the usual babble. Mom and Dad grilled me about school (with Gwen answering for me half the time), and traded remarks about their business as they happened to spring to mind.

We were all having a great time, until I asked Dad if he would drive me and Gwen to the movies and then pick us up. He said he couldn't. He said, 'I'm going out.' *Out*. No explanation. Mom flashed him the meanest look I'd ever seen. That was it, that ended dinner. Dad left, and Mom went upstairs, leaving me and Gwen and clawless Betty with a big mess to clean up. It happened so fast, I didn't even have a chance to ask Dad where he was going. No one did, not even Mom. Unless she already knew.

After a while, I went upstairs to see if Mom wanted some ice cream, and her door was closed. They never closed their door unless they were sleeping. I stood there for a minute, debating whether or not to knock. It was too quiet; something was wrong, besides Betty. Was that Mom crying? Why would she want to cry?

I didn't knock. I just crept downstairs to Gwen. She was sitting at the kitchen table eating directly out of the container of Heavenly Hash with a serving spoon.

*What was happening to our family?*

'Does she want any?'

I shook my head and sat down across from her.

'Good.' She licked the spoon.

I had always felt joined to Mom and Dad by an invisible cord. Ours had been a happy home, full of humor and sharing and learning and *quality time* before everyone else's parents both worked and they had to invent the phrase. *We* invented it. Mom and Dad were always dashing around in suits, with their fat briefcases, throwing me kisses on the run. I never felt neglected. Until Grove, until now.

Where had Dad gone?

'Hey, Kate,' Gwen said. 'I'm sorry you feel so bad. But like I told you, they sent you away for a reason.'

'What is it?'

She shrugged. 'I dunno.'

'I swear, they never acted like this before.'

'Yeah, tell me about it.' She leaned forward and grinned. 'Let's take a walk.'

'I don't feel like it.'

'You will.'

I didn't know what was on her mind, and I didn't much care. I felt so down all of a sudden, like a blind girl in the wrong house without her cane. So I let Gwen lead me outside. It was chilly and dark. There were no lights on our street, just big, sulky houses with blinking yellow windows. It was quiet and peaceful. We walked around the bend, out of sight of our house.

'Shh, just look at this,' Gwen whispered. She dug into her back pocket and withdrew the fat white joint she had showed me the first time we met. 'Yes?' she said. 'Okay? Now?'

I didn't know. I felt so down, I wanted to join that dark-cave club — any club — and not feel alone. I didn't know what grass would do to me, which is why I'd never smoked it before. The crazy thing was that now I didn't care.

So we smoked. We sat behind a bush in a neighbor's yard, and puffed away at our bitter weed. In no time, we were stupid. Then, when the high lifted us, everything seemed hilarious and we thought we were just about the funniest people alive. Then we had to eat, and it had to be something sugary, so we went home and stuffed ourselves on ice cream, raisins and cinnamon toast — whatever we could find. After, we went to the living room and lay head-to-foot on the couch and *passed out,* as they say in the trade.

Next thing I knew, it was morning. I sort of enjoyed the weird, hungover, cotton-brained feeling when I woke up at around ten o'clock. I remembered Dad sneaking in very late — or early — and felt wise and bitter and scared and revenged. Getting stoned was getting back. Mom and Dad were pulling off into their secret worlds, so I pulled off into mine.

Gwen made coffee while I made eggs, sausages and toast. I put the radio on loud, hoping the music would wake them. I was raring for a fight. Every few minutes, I raised the volume a little more. After a while, Dad came down. He was wearing his old blue bathrobe that Mom and I had given him one Father's Day, and a pair of worn leather mocassins. He yawned, stretched and crumpled onto a chair.

'Didn't get much sleep,' he said.

I poked the sausages and they sizzled.

'Coffee, Mr Steiner?' Gwen lifted the pot as if he needed a visual aid to stimulate his imagination.

'Yes, please.'

I gave her a mug and she poured. She was setting it down in front of him when Mom came in. She looked pretty in her ruby-red robe, with her long hair messy down her back like tangled vines. Her eyes looked watery and small, as if they stung.

'Morning, Mom!' I said.

'Morning.' She patted my waist on her way to the coffee pot.

'Have a seat,' Gwen said. 'I'm here to serve you.'

Dad chuckled, and Mom shot him a sharp look that stunned us all into silence. She pulled a chair out from the table very slowly, and it scraped like fingernails on a chalkboard. Dad cringed but Mom didn't even blink. She sat on the chair and rode it back under the table with two thuds.

'Something's burning!' Gwen said, hurrying to the stove. It was the sausages. They had sizzled nearly into oblivion.

'I like my sausages well done,' Dad said.

'Mom?'

'Just coffee for now, dear.'

Gwen stacked toast on a plate and put it in the middle of the table, and I served up the sausages and eggs.

'What are your plans for the day?' Mom asked me.

'I guess we'll go downtown.'

'We'll have dinner at about seven.'

She usually went to the office on Saturdays and worked. Dinner would be pizza and chocolate cake, a meal I looked forward to.

'That's okay, Mom, you don't have to cook.'

'I want to. I'm staying home today anyway.' She looked directly at Dad. 'I thought I'd go through the attic, get rid of some old junk.'

'Moll?' Dad said softly.

'It's just too cluttered around here.' Her voice was arctic-cold.

Gwen and I wandered around town. The sky was overcast and it was starting to get chilly. We ducked into stores for warmth: CVS, Toy Town, the florist, Woolworths. Gwen bought a red plastic ashtray, because no one in my parents' house smoked, and a box of catnip for Betty. I bought a small frame for a photo I had of Patrick in a striped sweater, smiling and waving at me. I called it the 'Hello Goodbye' picture. When I first had it developed, I would look at it and feel he was greeting me. Now when I looked at it, I felt a sharp pang of loss. I tried to tell myself that things were much harder for him than for me, that my suffering over him was nothing compared to his suffering over himself. If he *was* an addict, I could handle it; our love would heal him if only we had the chance. I kissed his photo and slipped it into the frame while we were standing on line. The price tag — $1.10 — covered half his face. I peeled it off before the cashier rang up the sale.

When we went back outside, it was raining. 'Bummer!' Gwen said. 'So, like, what do you want to do now?'

'Go home, I guess. I want to call Patrick. Rates go down after five.'

'Is it safe to go back yet?'

'Safe?'

'Yeah, you know, *safe* as in we won't get electrocuted by bolts of marital lightning.'

I wanted to say *nothing is wrong at home!* But I knew that wasn't true.

When we got back to the house, all was quiet. Mom was still upstairs in the attic. Dad was still out. Gwen sat on the living room couch and rubbed catnip into her sock. I called Patrick's mother's house. As the phone rang and rang, I watched Betty stalk Gwen's wiggling toes as if they were a litter of baby mice nestled under a blanket. Betty got wackier each time she sniffed the catnip, until eventually she hopped around in a frenzy. Meanwhile the phone rang twenty-seven times. I counted.

'No answer.'

'I'm not surprised.'

'He's probably at work.'

'Sure.'

'Well, you don't know where he is, either,' I said. 'Does a person have to be home all the time for you to believe they're telling the truth?'

Gwen believed that 'once a junkie, always a junkie'. She liked Patrick, but thought I was fooling myself by believing in him at all. I was tired of her cynicism. The way I saw it, faith was half the battle. The one time I said that to her, she responded that too much faith was just the mountain before the valley, the high before the crash. Though that wasn't how she put it. What she said was: 'Fuck that shit.'

Mom came downstairs in a pair of old bluejeans and a plaid shirt. Her hair was in a long braid down her back. I thought she looked great that way, like a girl, and told her so.

'Well, I'm not exactly young anymore,' she said, smiling. 'Come on, girls, give me a hand with dinner.'

We followed her to the kitchen.

'Just three plates,' Mom said, as I was about to lay out four. 'Dad's staying late at the office.'

'But it's Saturday night.'

'He has a case coming up. He'll grab a sandwich in town.'

Gwen shot me an *I told you so* look.

That was too much. 'Mom,' I said, 'where is he?'

She ignored me. 'How would you like to go to the movies tonight, all of us?'

All three of us, she meant. No Dad.

So, after dinner, we got into the silver Volvo and went to town. The movie was about funnyman Lenny Bruce, how he got famous telling dirty jokes that were nasty but true, and fell in love, and wrecked it all with drugs. In the end, of course, he died. It was a good movie but I hated it. A moralistic story about living wrong and ruining your life was the last thing I was in the mood for, considering the state of my life. Mom and Dad with a million miles between them. Patrick God-knew-where doing God-knew-what. Poor Patrick. If only I knew where he was, I'd go and save him, I wouldn't just run away like Lenny's wife, sitting in a cheap hotel in a puddle of tears.

I couldn't wait to get home to try calling him again.

It was just past eleven when we drove up to the house. We always left one downstairs lamp and the upstairs hall light on when we went out. Now, the windows of Mom and Dad's bedroom were bright yellow and you could see the flickering blue t.v. shadows inside.

Dad was home.

Mom slammed the brakes and we lurched forward. Without saying a word to us, she marched inside the house.

We slipped in quietly after her. Gwen turned on the tube in the living room and pretended to watch an old Claudette Colbert movie, but I don't think she was really paying attention. She was upset by what was happening. So was I.

I never knew I could feel so lonely in my own house. I dialed Patrick again, *wishing wishing wishing* . . . but he wasn't home.

Very late, after I'd been in bed awhile but still couldn't sleep, Dad crept into my room. Gwen was on the floor in a sleeping bag, snoring away. Dad stepped over her, and stood by the bed, looking at me. I pretended to be asleep. He bent down and kissed my forehead. It was not a normal goodnight kiss, but a *goodbye* kiss: long and heavy and sad. He left the room like a shadow, vanished.

There was no way I could sleep now. My room was full of an electric charge, a white sizzle of questions. *Where was Dad going? Why didn't he talk to me about it? Was Mom leaving, too?*

I couldn't stay in bed, so I put on my yellow robe and moccasin slippers, and went to their room to see if they were there. I thought maybe it had been a bad dream, maybe they were snuggled up in bed together. They didn't even have to be snuggled, they just had to be there.

But they weren't; the bed hadn't even been turned down. Their old green and blue bedspread was a little rumpled, that was all. Lights were on. It was too quiet. Until, outside, a motor revved. I looked out the window and saw Dad's blue Audi roll away.

'Mom? *Mom?*' I called.

There was no answer, no sound. So I went looking.

The attic door was open. The old wooden stairs glowed from the light of a weak overhead bulb. I'd always hated the sour smell of the attic, and now it seemed suffocating. But I went up anyway; I had to see who was there.

Mom was bent over a trunk. It looked like she was searching for something inside. I felt a surge of hatred for this woman I'd always loved, and my thought was: *she has driven him away.*

'What happened?' I said.

She didn't turn around. I could see by the way her back moved that she was breathing in spasms.

'What are you doing?'

Where she knelt over the trunk, there was no light, only shadows swimming with suspended dust. I watched her, and my anger cooled. It was as if she emitted some kind of force that changed my anger into shame. The soft curve of her back, the wave of her hair as it fell into the trunk, struck me as the saddest thing I had ever seen. I didn't hate Mom. I couldn't. I was so confused.

I knelt down next to her. 'Mom?' I whispered. 'Are you okay?' Her head moved but I couldn't tell whether it was a nod or a shake.

I looked into the trunk. When I was younger, this was my treasure chest, full of intriguing mysteries. I would come up here and study the articles of my parents' pasts. Now, to my surprise, I saw some of my own things. Someone must have put them there —Mom, probably — since I'd gone away to Grove. It was eerie seeing traces of myself mixed with the things of their histories. A converging of our lives, a time capsule. The trunk struck me now as too much a thing of memory, something static, dead.

'What are you looking for?'

Finally, she raised her face. Her expression was hard, detached from the past. Or maybe it wasn't her face that looked that way, maybe it was her eyes. I stared into a darkness and depth, a hollowness that echoed pain. She tried to smile but all she could manage was a vague shifting of the muscles around her mouth.

The trunk was lined with white paper printed with tiny

blue flowers. Orange stains, probably from rain and rusty hinges, formed scalloped patterns around the edges and in the corners. All the things in the trunk were neatly folded and stacked. A small-waisted red dress with white stripes. A pair of red shoes with pointed toes and thin high heels. Dad's fraternity pennant. A book they'd shared in college. Their letters of acceptance into the same law school. The lease of their first apartment. A tiny silver cup with my name engraved on both sides. A bundle of my report cards. Photographs of the family. Pieces of ribbon and string. The brochure of a ski lodge in Vermont where we'd spent a long weekend nine years ago. My eyes stopped at an envelope with my handwriting, addressed to Mom and Dad. It was a letter I'd written only recently from Grove.

How many hours had Mom spent hunched over this trunk? And why?

I put my arm around her, and she jerked away. Her head swung down toward the trunk, and her back moved in waves that alternated with a choking sound. She vomited. It didn't stop until she was empty, spent. I was repulsed by the sour smell, by the sight of Mom sick and helpless, by the vomit covering the remembrances in the trunk. But I couldn't leave her there alone, I just couldn't. The more she vomited the more I loved her. I felt that I loved her more deeply than ever before, as a woman, and as a woman who was my mother. My knees hurt from kneeling on the hard wood floor, but I didn't move. I held her forehead with my hand, hoping that in some way I was helping her, if not as a friend then at least as her child.

There is an underlying truth to every story. When Dad left Mom, I felt that my whole childhood had been a lie. Or, at least my interpretation of it. But that's the thing about childhood: the adults in your life present a smooth, easy picture, and then when you reach a certain age (depending on the family) they sock it to you. *The truth.* What their life together had really been like all along. The lies, the deceptions, the gaps in trust. How they held together for you, or didn't — they would say couldn't — despite their better judgement. The bottom line, they say, is that they still and will always love you, which had been an understanding and now becomes a dubious, often repeated statement to bolster your troubled spirit. Because suddenly, starting on the day they are sucked off in different directions, their truth turns inside out into your truth. Their ending is your beginning.

# FIVE

It was late when we arrived back at school on Sunday night. I was tired and depressed and could have sat in that bus all night long, gone all the way to China, buried myself in the ocean, for all I cared. I hated the thought of being back at Grove, without Patrick, and without a home to look forward to anymore. How had Gwen known so fast — the day she met me — that this was going to happen to my life? Poor Gwen. It was sad to know so much, so soon, before you've had a chance to really live. She didn't trust anyone, not really. Would I end up that way?

Gwen was asleep next to me, or I thought she was. As the bus's weight leaned into the curving driveway to the parking lot, she bolted up in her seat and said, 'Yo!' Leaning over, she whispered in my ear: 'It's Patrick!'

She pointed to the lawn next to the concrete parking lot, and there he was, Patrick, springing up from the ground.

I pushed my way off the bus and ran to him. He opened his arms and caught me in a hug.

'Surprise,' he said. 'I got back in!'

'When? How long have you been here?'

'Since yesterday. It took me fucking hours to convince the man to give me a chance. I missed you, Kate.'

'I've got your suitcase!' Gwen called out as she passed us.

She had one of the Little Kids lugging both our suitcases as well as his own enormous knapsack. She winked.

'I missed you too,' I said, 'a lot.'

He put his arm around me, and we walked up to the dorms.

'How was your weekend?' he asked.

'My parents are splitting up.'

Patrick stopped walking and looked down at me. He seemed so tall all of a sudden. Or maybe I just felt especially short.

'Are you sure?'

I nodded. 'I don't know why they had to wait till I got home to do it. Dad left last night. Mom's a real mess. Guess he's had a girlfriend for a while.'

'A girlfriend?'

'Almost a whole year, Mom said. A secretary. I can't believe it. Dad doesn't do stuff like that.'

'I guess he does.'

'No, I don't think so. I think there must be some kind of mistake.'

Patrick hugged me and I started to melt. I did feel pretty icy, almost cracked. I just couldn't picture Dad with someone else; he wasn't that sort of man; he was *good*, not *bad*. My dad wasn't so greedy that he'd abandon his family for another woman. And if he was, then I didn't know him, and he could just forget about me.

'Come on, Kate,' Pam called. 'Get inside!' Pam was an Upper Girls dorm parent who took her job way too seriously. 'It's past curfew! Get to your dorms!'

'Can't we have a few minutes together?' Patrick said. 'We haven't seen each other — '

'No.' She gave us one of her ugly bug-eyed glares.

'It won't be so bad,' Patrick whispered. 'I'll be here for you. Remember, I love you.'

So much for reunions. The machine of Grove had clicked on, and we were drawn into the routines of our respective dorms.

In the morning, as we walked down the hill toward lower campus and breakfast, Patrick told me as much as he could about what had happened to him.

'I locked myself in my room for three days. Jesus, my room got beat up! I was either jumping out of my skin or lying on my bed in convulsions. Three days and two nights. It was hell, it really was. Then, when it was over, my mother told my father about it right in front of me. He came over to see me, and she stood there and she said, "Your son is a heroin addict." She said *your son,* like I wasn't her son, too. My father said he couldn't let me stay with him, so my mother said she'd keep me if she had to. I don't know, Kate, I couldn't help it, I went out and —'

We reached the dining room. It was just before eight and the whole school was huddled in front of the door. The chilly November air was pressing in on us. What would it be like waiting to be let in for meals in the dead of winter?

'I couldn't help it,' Patrick whispered. 'It was just like that, I couldn't stop myself. I kept thinking about you, and it almost held me back.' He kissed my ear.

'But you stopped?'

'I did. I signed up with a program at the hospital. It was great. They —'

The dining room door swung open and we were swept up by the inrushing tide.

'Listen,' Patrick managed to say, 'I had to make a promise to Silvera when he let me back into school. Don't be surprised.'

It was too soon for most people to know Patrick was back. Our old seats together were already taken by the time we got into the dining room, and we had to sit at different tables. All during breakfast, I was dying of curiosity about Patrick's deal with the man.

Finally, after breakfast, Silvera said there was an announcement. Two tables over, Patrick stood up. The room broke into applause, welcoming him back. He hooked his thumbs into his belt loops, his shoulders sloped and his head hung slightly forward. He looked at me and smiled nervously. He cleared his throat.

'Well!' His voice cracked. 'Well, hi!' There was more applause. 'It's good to be back. I've missed school a lot.'

I couldn't believe it. Patrick wasn't exactly a renegade, but he also wasn't a Grover — one of those lackluster fools who played by the party-line without thinking. This speech must have been part of the bargain he made to get back into school.

'After classes —' Patrick's voice cracked again and he looked at me. I smiled. 'After classes this afternoon, there's gonna be sign-up for activities for the new quarter. I'm announcing a new one that I'll be running. It's called Drug Group and I hope anyone who feels they need to talk about drugs will join.' He glanced at me, then sat back down.

Drug Group. What was that? An assembly to *do* drugs, to *stop* doing drugs, or to trade war stories? I had heard kids talking: 'Man, I was *wasted*.' 'It really fucked me up.' 'It blew my mind.' I could just see a Grove Drug Group, run by Patrick: he could illustrate the discussions by showing the rash of tracks up his inner arms. Someone else could instruct as to alternate methods and territories: behind the knees, or under fingernails where the tracks wouldn't show.

Later Patrick told me, 'It was Silvera's idea. He said if I get five kids to sign up for a group about drugs, I can stay at school. All we have to do is talk about drugs.' He shrugged. No sweat. 'If fewer than five kids sign up, then I have to leave.'

'I'll join,' I said, 'and I'll ask Gwen. What about Eddie? That's three right there.'

He shook his head. 'You have to sign up for something else. Silvera specifically said so. Besides,' he smiled coyly, 'you're straight as an arrow. What do you know about drugs?'

'More than you think. Plus, I know *you*.'

'Ha ha. Cute. But Gwen can join if she wants to.'

'And Eddie.'

'Eddie can't.'
'Why not?'
'He's on probation.'

That was the first I'd heard that Eddie was in trouble. I looked over at him: he was standing near us, with John, Troy and Janice. Janice had a long face, a barely developed chest and slightly bowed legs. She was very thin, and with her long dark hair and black leather skirt, she looked tough — or at least like she wanted to. She and Troy pretended they were a motorcycle gang. I couldn't imagine them kissing. Troy was peeling bark off a stick, while Janice and Eddie threw stones at Peter Prentice. He was the one with the wacky idea to build a geodesic dome. Peter stood about ten feet away, board-straight, with his arms folded tightly over his chest. Every time a stone sailed past, he swayed in the other direction and then centered himself again, like one of those blow-up punch bags that bounce back after every hit. He was doing his Zen. And smiling.

'Poor Peter Prentice,' I said.

Patrick shrugged. 'We all have our problems.'

'Do you think he'd join your group?'

'I don't think he uses drugs. He's high on life, you know?' I laughed.

'But I bet Troy and Janice would, and maybe John. Come on.'

We marched over and enlisted them into Patrick's Drug Group. They liked Patrick, thought he was cool because he was an addict, a *junkie*. They were dead-end kids and admired defeat.

Activities sign-up was on the second floor of the school building, in a classroom across from Silvera's office. Pieces of green paper, one for every activity, were taped onto the blackboard. Already seven people had signed up for Drug Group! Gwen's was the first name; she'd promised to enroll the minute I told her John was joining too. I felt left out, having to choose a different activity for myself. I read the sheets over and over, and couldn't decide.

'How about Stained Glass? Louise is teaching it,' Patrick said.

'Nah. I still can't throw a pot on the wheel.'

'How about — ' Patrick was saying, when Silvera barged in. He walked back and forth, studying the green sheets, then stopped to write something on one of them.

'There you go,' he said. His face didn't budge; he just looked at me for a moment, then made a bee-line back to his office across the hall.

Patrick read the sheet Silvera had just signed, and laughed.

'What?'

'Come look.'

I went up to the blackboard and saw my name scribbled under Eddie's.

'I mean, I haven't even — '

'Go ask him why.'

'He's just trying to humiliate me!'

'Go ask him.'

'I will.'

I walked across the hall and rapped on the open door. Silvera was sitting in his rocking chair. A big smile forced his cheeks out and his face looked even fatter than usual.

'Why did you sign me up for that activity?'

'What activity?'

'*Sex Group.*'

Silvera shrugged. 'Why not?'

So, I found myself in Sex Group, angry at Silvera, and unwilling to contribute to the group in any way. The group leader was Ted, one of my dorm parents, and that made it even worse. Was I supposed to reveal my feelings about carnal knowledge, and my personal experiences (of which I had none) to a group of kids I hardly knew, and also to a man who saw me walking around in my nightgown with pimple medicine dotted on my face? My reticence was interpreted by the six-member group as hostility. I was only fifteen, but everyone assumed Patrick and I had slept together. When they badgered me into talking to them, during the fourth session, I came right out and told them I was a virgin.

'Bullshit!' Eddie said.

Because Eddie was Patrick's roommate, everyone believed him.

'I am!' I told them.

Ted crooked an eyebrow. He was small and chubby and cute, with curly brown hair and a frizzy beard. He reminded me of a koala bear. 'Why don't you tell us how you *feel* about that?'

'That would make her eligible to marry royalty,' said Rawlene, the tiny Be Here Butterfly.

'Yes,' Ted said gently, 'I suppose it would. But what we want to know here is how she feels about her virginity.'

I admitted that, despite peer pressure, I felt just fine about my innocence. Again, I was not believed.

I gave Gwen detailed reports of Sex Group. She thought that anyone who would sign up for one had to be too hung-up to believe sex or sexlessness could be that simple for someone else. She told me that in Drug Group, everyone had enough experience to know the lingo and they got into exciting, slang-ridden debates. I imagined Gwen often led them.

As the days passed, Patrick became noticeably happier. He said that Drug Group had been a good idea, that it was helping him. He would roll up his sleeves and show me his fading tracks. There were thousands of them, or at least that was how it seemed to me. Standing under the lamp at the end of the Boys Dorm fence, we counted. There were thirty-seven tracks on one arm, twenty-four on the other, thirteen behind one knee and nineteen behind the other. That made ninety-three. But Patrick said we might as well round it off to a hundred: he'd stuck needles under his fingernails a few times, too. One hundred ups! (One hundred downs!) We watched the red pinpricks blend gradually into his skin. One night — I don't know what took hold of me — I knelt down and kissed the insides of both his arms. He whispered, 'It's beautiful, you're poetry,' and lifted me up and hugged me. He tilted his hips slightly forward, and for the first time I felt his erection, hard and long, pushing at me through both our jeans.

One day in Sex Group, Ted had us draw our feelings about sex on the blackboard. Rawlene drew a wedding cake over in the corner. Laura drew a young girl standing alone in outer space, with her hair falling over her whole face except for her chin, which bore a large squirting zit. Alan from Upper Boys sketched the Pentagon in winter: two rotund snowmen guarding either side. Ted drew a pair of holding hands. Eddie made a drawing of a naked couple copulating right in the middle of the board. I drew outlines of hearts in all the free spaces. Suzie Zuckerman just scribbled.

When we were through, we sat in a circle on the floor.

Eddie said, 'I want to ask Kate what all those fucking stupid little outlines of hearts are supposed to mean. Like, I was wondering if she has some kind of problem or something, you know?'

I rolled my eyes. What a *jerk*.

Rawlene stuck her chin out and spat, 'What are you, some kind o'asshole, Edward?'

Ted shook his head. 'Eddie, I'd like to understand your feelings about Kate's drawings. But I'd also like to point out that what you just said was not only a value judgement, but unkind.'

Eddie shrugged. 'So?'

From Laura's usually silent spot in the group came a sob. Rivulets of mascara ran down her pale face. 'I wish everyone would leave Kate alone!' she said. 'She has enough problems!'

'Bitch,' Eddie said.

'I hate you, Eddie!' Laura said.

Ted observed the exchange with interest, but didn't say a word.

Finally Eddie just came out and said what was on his

mind. 'Patrick wouldn't be so frustrated if Kate wasn't such a prig.'

I was furious. Eddie was a slanderer; he didn't have any idea what he was talking about. 'Patrick never pressures me!' I said. 'He's never even asked me to sleep with him!'

Eddie's chubby face pinched up like a nasty prune. 'He shouldn't have to ask,' he said.

'That's enough,' Ted said. 'Kate, how do you feel right now?'

I felt lousy. I was dying to curse Eddie out, but then I would have gotten into trouble. So I said, 'I guess Patrick is a little horny.'

'Has he expressed it to you?'

I nodded.

'How?'

My eyes went to Eddie, who gloated mercilessly. My mind ran through possible answers, ranging from truth to diplomacy to lies.

I said, 'I could just feel it.' Literally, the truth.

Another truth: I didn't want to have sex — I wasn't ready — but it didn't take long for my innocence to shame me. I should have been proud of it — I could have, were it not for Grove. The place said NO while the kids said YES and my insides whirled I DON'T KNOW I DON'T KNOW I DON'T KNOW. I must have been the only virgin in the whole school. Pressure was on from every corner: Silvera, Eddie, Patrick, Gwen. To them, talk of sex was routine; to me, it was baffling and threatening and I would have preferred the safest sex available, which, as they now say, is no sex at all. But I couldn't avoid it anymore; they wouldn't let me.

# SIX

It was all around me. In Gwen's rain boot, in Eddie's dreams, in Patrick's memory, in Dad's new life. When Thanksgiving rolled around, I had to face it.
Sex.
Dad had a girl — not me, but a young woman who was his lover. They lived together, shared a bed; *she* was making the turkey this year. I didn't want to go, but they said I had to. The deal was Thanksgiving with Dad and Christmas with Mom. Mom's was the more important holiday — Christmas and Hannukah and New Year's Eve rolled into one — and I wanted to spend it with her. I had to give Dad something.
I invited Patrick to come with me for Thanksgiving, to guard and teach me. I had to grow up fast now, to learn about worlds I was entering without plan or warning, conquer the rules, defend myself.
Gwen was going to an aunt's in northern New Jersey. 'They call it The Other Switzerland,' she said. 'Lots of hills and lakes and stuff. It's real pretty. Plus, they've got cute guys and bars.'
'You're under age,' I said. 'You couldn't get in.'
'Sure I could. One of my cousins makes fake ID's.'
'You should be careful.' I was standing over my open

suitcase. I had packed a couple pairs of jeans and a few shirts and couldn't think of what else I'd need.

'Don't you know how to have fun?' she said. 'You better bring a dress or something in case they take you out. I mean *really*.'

'I don't want to go out with them.'

'You'll regret it. I love eating in restaurants.' She rushed to the closet and got her high heels.

'Remind me to take my hairbrush and toothbrush,' I said.

'I hope Patrick's bringing some rubbers. I mean, he's coming home with you, right? *Coming*.' She grinned.

'You know Patrick and I don't do that.'

'Maybe you should, is all I'm saying.' She fished her black negligée out of her rainboot in the closet. 'You never know,' she said, tossing it at me in a silky flutter. I tossed it back.

But somehow, I would discover, she managed to slip it into my bag. I didn't *take* the negligée, as Silvera would later claim. I didn't plan any of it. It just happened, step by step, innocently, like most anti-events that twisted minds distort into scandal. Nothing happened over Thanksgiving vacation. We met Dad's girlfriend, ate the usual turkey, and — okay — I slipped into the first sex-skin of my life, and it was black, and it *was* Gwen's negligée. But that was all; it was nobody's business what happened between Patrick and me. We loved each other. What we did or didn't do together was private, or should have been.

Dad leaned against the wall opposite our gate at the bus terminal, waiting. Even after he spotted me, he just stood there and watched us. He smiled. I stared at him. He was wearing jeans and a translucent yellow Indian shirt over a black turtleneck. His hair was long. He looked silly, like an old man trying to be young. I liked him much better in his suit and tie.

'You must be Patrick,' he said.

Patrick thrust his hand nervously into Dad's, and they shook. 'Nice to meet you, Sir.'

Dad liked that. *Sir*.

'His name's Max,' I said.

Patrick glanced at me, then said to Dad, 'I really appreciate the invitation.'

'We're glad to have you.'

There he went with the *we*. The sound of it squeezed my stomach; I felt sick just thinking about it. We. Her.

'Well,' Dad said. 'Shall we?'

Patrick nodded and looked at me.

I said, 'Shall we what?'

'Go home,' Dad said.

'Home? Oh, right.'

Patrick shot me an *oh Kate* look, a look that said *can it, willya, and give the guy a chance.*

'Yeah, okay.' I sighed. And Patrick shook his head at me. But Dad only smiled.

Dad was even more scared than I was! He was no dope; he knew what he'd done to our family. It must have embarrassed him to do such a stereotypical thing as to run off with a younger woman. Not that he ran very far: they were living in the city, in an old Upper West Side apartment. He was trying to differentiate himself, to jazz it all up with Indian clothes and long hair, to turn it into some kind of romantic adventure. He had his arm around Patrick's shoulders and I knew Dad was really confused. He was trying too hard. He couldn't afford *not* to like Patrick, and that was to be our barter system: the more points he scored by me — giving me things, liking my friends, allowing me freedoms — the more tolerance I owed him. Already, with Patrick, he was setting me up with a debt of generosity, trying to earn my acceptance of *her*.

Her name was Lisa. Their apartment had one bedroom, a kitchen and a living room which led into a kind of turret that housed her piano. The turret was lined with small windows of old thick glass through which twilight poured magnificently. Maybe because it was *her* piano, because *she* was the one who played it, I hated that turret. It was simple and beautiful, unencumbered, bright in the morning and richly colorful in the evening. It was hers, my father's mistress, the destroyer of our family.

In describing Lisa, Mom had exaggerated in the negative. Lisa was a woman, not a girl. She supported herself as a secretary, but was also an accomplished pianist. She was a little shorter than average and plump in a voluptuous kind of way. She had wavy blond hair and pale blue eyes. I would catch Dad looking at her as if he wanted to touch her, which he never did in front of me. I was glad. I had no desire to play the generous, understanding daughter. It was bad enough seeing their quaint little set-up, their home. Blatant affection would have only twisted the knife in the wound.

I didn't like Lisa for what she represented in my life, and she clearly didn't like me, maybe for what I represented in Dad's life. She treated me with an insidious hostility which only I could detect. That was smart of her. To Dad, she was the kind sort-of-stepmother to his daughter. To me, she was the plunderer of rights. It was as if I were the intruder, not her. I was tempted to tell her, straight out, that she had it backwards. Gwen would have told her. But not Patrick. He didn't see it as clearly as I. He thought I was exaggerating when I tried to tell him how unwelcome she was making me. He couldn't taste the poison in her onslaught of gourmet cooking. She must have believed that old cliché that the way to a man's heart was through his stomach, because she had both of them, Dad and Patrick, enthralled.

She had all the meals worked out in advance. There were flowers everywhere. She had marked all the good movies listed on t.v. through Sunday. But she wouldn't look me in the eye.

Dad and Lisa invited some of their friends over for Thanksgiving dinner. That was another thing: *their* friends. I knew that they'd had this apartment together for nearly five months before Dad left Mom, but still, it shocked me to realize they had cultivated their own social life. Dad had had a whole other, secret existence from ours. I felt betrayed.

Who were these friends? Why did I have to meet them? They were all the enemy, against me, against Mom, against the reality of our old life together. I no longer had a real place in Dad's life; it was like he had flipped the channel mid-plot, and I was lost.

These friends were a couple from Manhattan — Vladimir, a Russian jewelry designer and Suzy, his American actress wife — and another man, a lawyer. His name was Jerry O'Haran and he was the only one I really liked.

Vladimir was big and tubby, with a scraggy beard that looked like pubic hair. Suzy was the opposite: small and neat with short black hair and perfectly ironed clothes. She was decked out in outrageous jewelry made by Vladimir. BIG stones set in BIG strips of gleaming gold or silver. It looked fancy and expensive and I hated all of it. Vladimir and Suzy were nice people, but I hated them too. They just didn't belong. No one did. Neither did I.

Patrick and I sat next to each other in chairs facing the couch, where Vladimir and Suzy were spread out, especially Vladimir. Dad was in the kitchen cooking, while Lisa played hostess. When she handed around wine glasses, she included Patrick and me. We looked at each other and shrugged. Normally, adults didn't serve alcohol to minors, especially kids like us who came from a place like Grove. She filled our glasses with wine, and we drank it. I liked the buzzy numb feeling I got before long; it took me out of my tension, into a zero-zone of not really caring.

No one noticed I was getting drunk, not Vladimir or Suzy or Dad or Lisa or even Patrick, no one but Jerry O'Haran. Maybe that was why I liked him. He was unaffected, silent and aware, sitting next to me without a young girlfriend in shining bracelets screaming stones. Jerry had thinning brown hair parted far over on the side, and wore wire-rimmed aviator glasses. He was dressed in brown pants, a tweed jacket and a white shirt, which struck me as dull but appropriate for his age — I guessed forty-five. It seemed to me he was the only normal adult in the room. He just leaned back in his chair, with his wine glass balanced on his knee, looking all around. I smiled at him, and he smiled back. He had twinkly brown eyes topped with these incredibly bushy eyebrows. He winked at me, and one eyebrow angled up.

Then he really surprised me. He said, 'I knew you when you were a baby.'

'You did?'

'Yup. You had red fuzz all over your head. You looked like a peach.'

'Do you know my mother?'

'Of course,' he said. 'I've known Max and Molly for almost twenty years. We were in law school together.'

Apparently he was on Dad's side, since he was here as a guest. Maybe I didn't like this Jerry so much, after all, not if he was one of Dad's conspirators in his secret life.

I was a little drunk, so it slipped right out, when I said, 'Well I think all this sucks.'

Jerry nodded. I didn't know if it was because he agreed with me, or wanted to shut me up. Suddenly I was angry. A storm was whirling up inside me and I wanted to run. But then Lisa marched in with a gigantic tray of hors d'oeuvres, and distracted us with explanations of what they were. The white roll was *chêvre* rolled in fresh pepper, the sickly beige lump was *foie gras,* the wrinkled black things were oil-cured Greek olives, and the pruny red stuff was sun-dried tomatoes in virgin olive oil and fresh herbs.

'I have potato chips for you,' she said to Patrick and me. He looked relieved. I was insulted. Then she said, 'But sorry, no dip.'

I hated her. I couldn't help it. 'I see one,' I said under my breath as she walked away.

Jerry smiled. And I knew: he was on my side.

Vladimir dug right into the bowl of potato chips. I kept hoping Lisa would notice, but every time she floated in and out of the room, he was nowhere near the bowl. She thought I was eating them all. When she refilled the bowl from a huge bag, she slid me a look that said *here you go, you nasty little glutton.*

Thanksgiving dinner was no better. We had turkey with wild rice and walnut stuffing, fresh stewed cranberries, new potatoes with dill, escarole salad, and kiwi pie. It tasted good, but it wasn't normal; it wasn't a real Thanksgiving dinner like we'd always had them, with chestnut stuffing, sweet potatoes, boiled onions, cranberry sauce, peas in butter, and homemade apple pie. Lisa's version had no history. I sat between Dad and Patrick. Every now and then Patrick would look at me and smile, with real love in his eyes, as if we were all alone. He could bolster me even with silence, his silences were so full. Dad kept looking at me, too, but with him it was different. Every time one of Lisa's creations came my way, he would slip me an understanding look. It was as if he knew in his gut exactly how I felt about everything from his woman to her food, that I didn't like them, that I couldn't fit into his new life.

I couldn't. I wouldn't.

Patrick and I slept on the living room floor in sleeping bags. We lay them down next to each other and crawled into our separate sacks. The only parts of us that touched were our hands, clasped loosely between us.

'Don't you think you were a little extreme?' he asked me.

'No.'

He let go of my hand, and I felt abandoned and cold. He rolled over, leaned on his elbow, looked at me. It was dark, but there was enough moonlight coming through the unshaded turret windows to see him. He reached over and smoothed my hair back from my forehead. 'You have to accept it,' he said softly. 'Your father made a choice. This is his home now.'

'I hate her.'

'You don't hate her,' he said. 'You hate your father living with her. That's different.'

'Not much.'

'It's different.'

'What am I supposed to do? She's so weird. She's nothing like Mom.'

'Shh. They'll hear you.'

'I don't care.'

'You'll hurt his feelings. Couldn't you see how sensitive he is about it? He's so scared you won't accept him now.'

I rolled my eyes. But I knew, inside, that Patrick was right.

'I know how you feel,' he said. 'I've been through it, remember?' His forehead was tense and his eyes were staring at me. I knew that look; he was worrying. I felt guilty for my selfishness in consuming his emotions like this, at stirring up tension and doubt. I had seen how fragile he was underneath all his calm. I had seen him shatter and fly away.

I rolled over so we were facing each other.

'Tell me,' I said.

'What?'

'That you know I love you a lot.'

He smiled. 'I know you love me a lot.'

'Swear?'

'Swear.'

He kissed me — a soft, luscious kiss — as his hand ran down along my back. My old flannel nightgown was thin enough for me to feel his fingers press into my skin. Chills danced up my back, and I shivered.

He hummed, 'Ummm,' and kissed me again.

'Roll over,' he said, 'I'll give you a back-rub.'

Maybe it was naive of me, but I was genuinely surprised when he raised my nightgown. I didn't resist. This was Patrick, my Patrick, and I trusted him. He looked at my breasts before turning me over. His hands felt warm and dry as they kneaded my back. I could feel myself relaxing; muscles I never knew I had turned to goop. When his fingers grazed the sides of my breasts, a tingle ran through my body and I realized how wet I was between my legs, and what it meant.

'How do you feel?' he whispered.

Smart, nervous remarks flitted through my mind, but I rejected all of them. How *did* I feel? I felt good! I felt *great*! I rolled over and stretched my arms above my head. He knelt over me, straddling my body, gazing watery-eyed at my bare moon breasts. I would give myself to him, in love, passion, adventure and trust. I would let him grow me up into a woman. Release me from my girl-self and my former life. Sex. I thought that was all it would take.

I closed my eyes and waited for him to do it, whatever it was; to begin me as a woman. He lowered himself over me, slowly, coming closer and closer, blanketing me with his shadow, until finally his lips touched my forehead.

Then he rolled back to his own sleeping bag, and whispered, 'Goodnight.'

Brunch the next morning was homemade blueberry pancakes covered in hot Vermont maple syrup mixed with sweet butter. Lisa was really going all-out to hook Dad completely. I suppose she wanted to marry him. Hot buttery syrup! Patrick kept throwing me looks that told me to act as if I liked it. Well, I did like it, but I didn't see why she should know. She had Dad. What else did she want from me?

Later, when Lisa went shopping and Patrick was blitzed out in front of the t.v., I stole some private time with Dad. He was reading in his bedroom. I sat on the edge of the bed.

'Dad,' I said, 'tell me about when you and Mom met.'

He looked up from his book. 'You've heard that story a hundred times.'

'I know, but I want to hear it again. *Please.*'

He set the book on his lap. 'Mom was standing on line to register for an English Lit class. I was on the next line, for a Philosophy class.' He stopped as if that was all, but I knew there was more to it.

'You couldn't stop looking at her.'

'That's right.'

'And she smiled.'

'Why do you need to hear all this again?'

'Because I like it. If you hadn't stood on those lines, I wouldn't exist.' The thought had always intrigued me.

'I can hardly believe you're almost sixteen years old.'

'When you asked Mom out, did she think about it, or did she say yes right away?'

'I don't remember.'

'She said yes, and you went to the cafeteria and had coffee.'

'Are you happy at school?'

'You and Mom got married three months after you met. You eloped.'

His eyes went dreamy, cloudy, wet. 'Our parents were furious,' he said. 'We were still in college. They thought we were ruining our lives. But we both finished college and we both went to law school. It wasn't easy, but we were happy and that made all the difference.'

'What do you see in *her*?'

The muscles in his face tensed instantly upon abandoning the memory. 'That's inappropriate,' he said.

'So?'

'Patrick's a nice boy.'

I felt a sudden urge to beat down any image he had of me as a know-nothing- good-little-girl. I said, 'He's a drug addict, Dad.'

He smiled and shook his head. He didn't believe me. Finally I left the room.

Patrick told me that the first year of divorce is the hardest, but that eventually you get so used to it, you can't even picture your parents together. I had completed the first month and could still barely picture them apart. Dad's new life was a determination against our old life. He was pulling himself out of the mental picture I tried to sustain of Mom and Dad together. He was putting himself in another picture, one that for me was impossible. So instead of granting him that, I would obliterate him. I would not succumb to the picture of my parents apart, but would allow him to fade out of the single picture of them together. I would abandon him to my past, stash him away in my memory.

I had to. My childhood had betrayed me. Now, growing up was the only thing left.

That night, I practiced wearing Gwen's black negligée, posing in front of the bathroom mirror, studying myself. I liked the sexy redheaded girl staring back at me. She was pretty. Her breasts were small and so were her hips and waist. The negligée had thin straps that flowed into lace and then silk. It came down to just above her knees, which looked a little knobby. Her hair sizzled over her pale freckled shoulders. The deep black of the silk accentuated her natural colors: the dark green of her eyes, the pink of her lips, the vivid orange of her hair, the white of her skin. She was the first image of a young woman I ever saw in myself. She looked at me straight in the eye, and smiled.

Dad and Lisa had gone to bed. I moved around the apartment nonchalantly, turning off lights. When I came into the living room, I deliberately didn't look at Patrick, who was half in his sleeping bag, staring at the t.v. I lay on top of my sleeping bag, crossed my ankles, and waited for him to notice.

He ignored me.

I giggled and rolled over, and finally he looked. His eyes were smiling, but his forehead was bunched with tension.

'Where did you get that thing?'

'It's Gwen's.'

He slid all the way into his sleeping bag and rolled over, away from me. A second later, he rolled back to face me.

'Would you marry me?' he asked. 'Theoretically, I mean.'

'Sure!'

'Good.' He rolled back over. 'As long as we understand each other.'

After a while, he started to snore in long, sawing breaths. I wasn't insulted. I knew he was doing this for me, that refusing the sex I offered him was his way of loving me. He had been through his own parents' divorce. He was older than me. He knew what highs were real, and when, and he knew enough to spot a quick escape. He was a master at quick escapes; just look at his arms. He loved me and didn't want me to learn to use escapes, too. Like sex. I really wasn't ready. And he knew.

# SEVEN

I was still a virgin when we got back from Thanksgiving vacation. I had mixed feelings about it. On the one hand, I was relieved, since virginity was all I knew and so it was comforting. But on the other hand, I was curious and wanted to know what waited on the other side, you know, the *inside* part of my body where sex would change me into a woman. I was still a girl. Which turned out to be just fine, since when the big scandal happened, no one could rightfully say that Silvera's accusations against me were true.

We all found out about it indirectly, through random comments and observations that surfaced like pieces of a puzzle bobbing up for air. Grove was a small place, and you couldn't hide anything, especially not the juicy stuff — and this was juicy.

For me, it started when Patrick asked me to deliver an envelope to Laura. It was a plain white envelope with her full name typed on the front. He said it was a love letter from one of the boys, and no one was supposed to know, and he couldn't tell me because he was sworn to secrecy. I accepted that. Kids were passing love letters for each other all the time. Even Patrick and I had couriers deliver letters when we were fighting or just wanted to be romantic. So I handed the envelope to Laura, and that was that. Then he gave me another letter for Alison. The next one was for Louise, and I assumed it was from Jimmy. That was all, nothing else happened, until Rawlene, Amy and Nicole got permission from the dorm parents, who got their permission from Silvera, to throw a party in Upper Girls to which selected boys would be invited. *Selected* boys meant boyfriends and whoever else would be considered an asset to the fun. I was elected to the party committee, along with Gwen, Janet (the oldest girl in the dorm), and Lee Lee (who was extremely disorganized but had a lot of enthusiasm). Rawlene, Amy and Nicole were too busy practicing the new Be Here Butterflies routine to help with the planning, even though the party was their idea.

Working on the party excused us from activities for two afternoons. That meant no Sex Group! As we planned, the Be Here Butterflies put on some *Earth Wind and Fire,* linked arms, and danced. They were in search of a new step. Every now and then they'd agree on a combination, and would practice it over and over. Then they'd trip over each other's feet for a while in search of the next move. Meanwhile, we sat on the floor in a corner of the lobby — our living room — drinking tea with honey and making executive decisions. The first thing we did was make a list of the boys we'd invite. Every official boyfriend was invited right off the bat, but there was some dissention as to whether we should also invite the boys who we knew as a fact to be in the process of mutual flirtation with one of the girls, or who were the unknowing objects of some girl's desire. The problem was that someone might be excluded who should have been included, and vice versa. Finally we decided to invite only actual boyfriends, but would also spread the word among the girls that special requests would be accepted.

The decor would be the best of the rock 'n roll posters from the girls' rooms, candles, and Gwen's lava lamp on the mantle piece. For refreshments we would serve pretzels, potato chips, onion dip, Wheat Thins, nut-rolled cheese ball, and fruit punch.

That night, before lights-out, we held a special meeting to announce our plans and ask for suggestions. We added carrot sticks to the menu, substituted Triscuits for Wheat Thins, and got permission to get the kind of cheese ball with streaks of red wine running through it. We told the girls that, as we'd be going to the mall tomorrow to get the supplies, they had until morning to put suggestions into the box on the mantle. This, we added, included special guest requests.

Seven slips of paper were left in the suggestion box. One said *John Reilly* in handwriting I recognized as Gwen's. I smiled when I saw the slip, and she punched my arm. After that, the word was out: Gwen liked John! Another slip contained a recipe for champagne punch using ginger ale instead of champagne, which we voted to use instead of fruit punch. Another slip said *Ford Highway* which we discounted as a joke. And the remaining four slips said the same thing: *Eddie Cohen, Eddie Cohen, Eddie Cohen, Eddie Cohen*. Two were hand-written in different inks, two were typed.

Eddie didn't have a girlfriend, and no sane girl would ever admit to liking him. We decided that since none of *us* liked him, since we all believed he would detract from the party, since we had trouble believing that four of our dormmates were infatuated with him, but since four slips had named him, we would cite ethical deadlock and put the matter to our dorm parents.

We met in Pam's room after classes, with Pam, Ted and Jimmy. Pam leaned against the radiator cover in her raspberry pantsuit which clung to all the wrong places such as her saddle-bag hips and stomach roll. Her arms were folded across her chest, and she tapped her foot nervously; her whole body seemed to say *let's get on with it*. Ted was at the other extreme, calm and patient, sitting on a chair in the corner, stroking his fluffy beard with stumpy fingers. Jimmy was Jimmy: smallish, thinnish, moderate, and unconcerned with how fast things got done.

Lee Lee, a pretty girl with thick black hair down to her shoulders, sat in the middle of the floor nervously removing and replacing her hair clip. Janet, tall and blond, stood over her. Gwen and I leaned against the door.

'So,' Ted began, 'what's up?'

'Oh, let's just invite him!' Lee Lee said.

Janet's forehead crunched. 'What?'

'What are we talking about, here?' Pam said.

'It's about the party,' I said.

Gwen said, 'It's about Eddie-the-asshole-Cohen.'

Jimmy laughed. 'Oh!'

'What about Eddie?' Ted asked. I just knew he was thinking back to Sex Group, to the outburst between Eddie and Laura. We all knew that Lee Lee was Laura's best friend.

Lee Lee shrugged.

'Lee Lee, why don't you tell us what this is all about,' Ted said.

'*I'll* tell you,' I said. I leaned forward and started to say, 'He — ' but Ted cut me off.

'I'd like to hear it from Lee Lee.'

Lee Lee shrugged. She looked embarrassed. 'I did it for Laura,' she said. 'She asked me to.'

Pam became interested. 'Did what?'

'Yeah,' I said. 'Did what?'

Janet knelt down and placed a hand on Lee Lee's shoulder. 'Did you put those slips in the box?'

Lee Lee nodded. 'But only two of them! She asked me to make sure he got invited.'

'I think I understand,' Ted said.

Suddenly I recalled what Patrick told me. 'Why is Eddie on probation?' I asked. And then I remembered the letters Patrick had asked me to deliver, and realized they must have been from Eddie. I didn't know what he was writing to these different girls, but since I'd delivered the letters, I thought it was time to keep quiet, and just listen.

'How did you know about that?' Pam said.

I shrugged.

'What's going on?' Janet said.

'Gwen,' Ted said, 'knock on Gene's door and ask him to come up here, please.'

'Sure,' she said, and left the room. She was too quiet; Gwen did not obey mysterious orders without asking why.

'And why don't you go get Laura,' he told Lee Lee.

Later, we were told that because Eddie's name had been put in the suggestion box, we had to invite him to the party. They knew all four slips were phonies. But we did as we were told.

By the time we had the party on Tuesday night, the whole dorm was abuzz with the mystery. No one, though, admitted to knowing what it was about. All I knew was that Eddie was on probation, and Patrick was acting as courier (and so was I!), and Gwen knew something too, and for some reason poor sad Laura was sending out *help* signals.

We decorated the lobby with streamers (a last minute thought), candles, the lava lamp and snacks. Gwen lit a stick of spicy incense. I had been begging her to fill me in on what was going on with Eddie, but all she would ever say was, 'Nothing.' And when I asked her if she had put the other two slips with Eddie's name in the suggestion box, she laughed hysterically and rolled her eyes and said, '*Oh please*,' but she didn't answer.

Patrick was the first boy to arrive. He had on his good jeans and a turqoise shirt that made a neon contrast with his orange hair. He looked so handsome. I wore a red sweatshirt, my oldest jeans and a choker of silver circles like connected infinity signs. I borrowed red lipstick from Gwen.

'You look great!' Patrick said. He kissed me, right there in front of all the girls. They whooped and cheered and clapped. He kissed me again. I felt like the luckiest girl in the whole dorm, and maybe, just for that moment, I was.

Soon the lobby was full of boys and girls and laughter and buzzing talk and music and dancing and smoke. That awful smoke! I had to escape to the hallway periodically to get away from it. Patrick would stay inside and have his cigarettes then.

I was sitting on the steps just outside the lobby door when Eddie appeared. I was surprised to realize he hadn't been at the party yet.

'Need a friend?' he said.

I shrugged. 'Not really.'

'Good,' he said, and sat on the step beneath me.

His face looked tight and shiny, like he'd just scrubbed it, and his wavy hair was slicked down.

'Where's Patrick?'

'Inside.'

'How's the party?'

'Why don't you go in, Eddie? You were only invited by about a million different girls.'

'Would you feel comfortable going in there if you were me?'

I shrugged. 'I don't know.'

Eddie looked at me straight-on, eye-to-eye. It was so unlike him, it disarmed me. I almost had a sense he could be trusted.

'I guess not,' I said.

He leaned back against my knees and said, 'Anyway, it's nice out here.'

I tried to get up, but he put his arms around my knees and started kissing them.

'Eddie, don't!'

He stopped abruptly and shook his head. 'I can't do this to Patrick.'

'Patrick? What about me?'

'Sorry,' he said, 'sorry.' Then he stood up, opened the lobby door, and disappeared into the cacophony of the party.

I went back inside to find Patrick. He was leaning against the wall near the door. I wanted to tell him what had just happened, but before I had a chance, he said, 'Look!'

The Be Here Butterflies stood in front of the fireplace in

matching red dresses trimmed with black sequins. They were lined up according to size: first Rawlene, then Nicole, then Amy. The music blasted HEY and they clapped and spun in place. They were perfectly synchronized, for once. They lunged, and swung their hips, and shimmied their shoulders. Nicole belted out Diana Ross's song: STOP! *in the name of love* . . . . Everyone was watching them. They were magnificent, more inspired than ever, this time really *with it*. Just when they were building up to their finale — arms spread, bosoms up — Eddie jumped in front of them and shimmied backward until his knees touched the floor. A roar of booing egged him on, and he jerked his hips forward. Rawlene landed a kick on his shoulder, and he toppled over to laughter and applause.

'What an ass,' I said.

Patrick looked at me steadily, deciding, I thought, whether or not to agree with me. I wanted him to break Eddie's trust and tell me why he was on probation, what was going on with Laura, everything. Patrick's face was a spot of intense quiet in the midst of all the noise. Finally he said, 'I dunno,' and shrugged.

Patrick knew something. There was a big secret and he was deliberately keeping it from me, and Eddie knew that and had jerked me around in the hall for fun. It may have been fun for him, but not for me; and it was even less fun to feel Patrick was lying to me by withholding some important truth. Why wouldn't he just tell me? What could be so bad?

I could see Gwen's silhouette in the dark. She was sitting on her bed, and each time she turned her face toward the window her somber expression was bathed in pearly moonlight.

'Gwen,' I whispered.

She didn't move; she was like a statue.

'*Gwen.*'

'Shh. Listen.'

I angled up on my elbows, and listened. First, it was all

silence. Then I heard voices in the lobby. There were at least three, maybe four.

'Who is it?' I whispered.

'*Shh.*'

She glided silently to my bed and sat down next to me. Leaning very close, she whispered, 'It's a conspiracy.'

Her hair tickled my face and I turned my head. She leaned toward me. 'They're going to turn him in.'

'Who?'

'*Shh*. They'll hear us.' Her breath grazed my cheek as she lay down next to me.

'But Gwen,' I whispered, 'what do you have to do with it?'

'Nothing and everything,' she said in a soft, throaty whisper. Then she mumbled, 'I'm sorry,' and fell asleep.

The next morning, I woke up and thought it was all a dream: Eddie on the stairs at the party, and then Gwen, later, so mysterious in our room. The shower was running, and when Gwen came out of the bathroom wrapped in a white towel, I asked her.

'What are you talking about?' She leaned over and shook out her wet hair.

'Who was in the lobby? Why were you upset?'

'You better get in the shower before it's too late.'

It was almost seven-thirty. 'Tell me later?'

'Okay.'

But *later* never materialized. Instead, she left it to Silvera to shock me along with everyone else that night.

After dinner, as always, Silvera stood to make announcements. He was wearing black polyester slacks, and a big red turtleneck over which his ever-present butterfly medallion hung like a badge of the wise. His hairy navel was visible between the end of his shirt and his belt buckle. He paced, his black eyes fixed intensely on the floor. He chewed his mustache and stroked his beard. He let the tension of his silence suffuse us. Then he stopped and turned around, his eyes jumping from table to table.

'School meeting at nine-fifteen!' he said. Then, curtly, 'Dismissed!'

School meetings were always bad. Routine matters were covered in after-meal announcements; special meetings to convene the whole school meant it had to be serious.

On the way up to the dorms to change for study hall, questions about the purpose of the school meeting were passed from person to person, couple to couple, group to group, like a stick in a relay race. No one had the answer, or would admit they did. By the time we all gathered in the dining room for the meeting, the whole school was buzzing with curiosity.

All the tables were pushed to the sides of the room, and chairs were scattered in a loose, layered circle. The room was filling up. Patrick and I hurried to find two seats together. We ended up by the door of the dishwashing room, where Crazy Hal stood in the doorway with a rag over his shoulder, his rotten tooth showing through his smile.

At exactly nine-fifteen, Silvera came through the kitchen door dragging a high stool. He placed the stool in front of the fireplace. It seemed logical that he had gone to all that trouble so he could sit on the stool himself, towering above everyone. But instead, he stood next to it.

'I love this school,' he said, 'I really love this school. And I love all of you, every single one of you.' He drew in his lips and his eyes rolled to the ceiling. A tear ran down his cheek. 'But damn it!' His voice was scratchy now. 'When I find out that you . . . That you. . .' He shook his head dramatically and paced once, back and forth, across the floor. 'That you *lie* to me, it hurts me. I don't ask for much. Do I? Do I really ask for so much? No, no, I don't think so. All I ask is honesty. But when you withhold things, when you play games and keep them secret, then every single thing you do or say every single minute is a lie. A lie. Because, if you're not completely honest all the time, then you are dishonest. You are dishonest if you withhold the truth. *You are a liar.*' He paced quickly now and his eyes flashed around the room.

'You!' He shouted, stopping suddenly and pointing at Louise. She stared back at him, stunned.

'And you!' He pointed at Eddie.

'And you, both of you, liars!' he shouted at Patrick and me.

My heart raced. I wished I knew what Eddie's letters had said. I stared into Silvera's black eyes, until he turned his attention elsewhere. When I looked at Patrick, I found him staring at the space abandoned by Silvera as if it were a ghost.

'What is this?' I whispered.

Patrick shook his head. Before he could speak, Silvera shouted:

'Kate Steiner! Kate! Come on, come on!' He slapped the stool.

I didn't move. I couldn't.

'Come here,' he said. 'Let's hear it from you.'

'What?' My voice sounded disembodied, high and weak. I felt dizzy. 'I don't understand.'

'*Bullshit.*' He stood there and glared at me. When I still didn't move, he came forward. His stomach bounced and his face looked big and grotesque, like a monster or a bad dream. This *was* a bad dream. I squeezed shut my eyes, terrified. He had slapped me once before and I never really understood why. This time, at least, I was ready.

I heard a chair scrape the floor and topple over. I opened my eyes. Patrick was standing in front of Silvera. Silvera's hands were on Patrick's shoulders, trying to push him aside. Patrick clenched his teeth and kneed Silvera in the groin. The man crumpled in pain.

Voices rose and a few people stood. But no one came forward. Patrick stood with his hands loose at his sides as if to indicate that he didn't intend to fight again. But I think he did. His face was white and angry; rage sparkled in his eyes.

Silvera was squeezing his thighs together, cradling his groin with a cupped hand. He lifted his other hand and ejected a straight fat finger. 'Get out!' he told Patrick.

'You're expelled! No grace period! Get what you need and leave immediately!'

Patrick's hands curled into fists and he lurched forward, poised to fight. 'You sick slob,' he said. 'I never wanted to be here anyway!'

'Ha! Then why did you come back?'

Patrick hesitated; his anger paused. He said, 'I had nowhere else to go.'

He was crying when he turned to me. He wove his way through the chairs to the front door. And was gone.

Patrick! But NO, I would not cry, not for the fat man. If I cried, he would have loved it, it would have fueled him in whatever his current crusade was. I pulled in my tears, recalled them, and stared right back at him, into those inkwell eyes.

'He's gone now,' Silvera said, 'you don't have to cover up for him.'

'What?'

He nodded quickly. In a low, controlled voice, he called, 'Eddie Cohen!'

Eddie sat by the front door, near Gwen. I hadn't noticed her before. She looked exhausted, pale, tense. Her eyes snapped away when she saw me looking at her. Her lips clutched together. She watched Eddie.

Eddie pretended not to hear Silvera. He stared mutely at his knees.

'Eddie,' Silvera said.

Walter, Lower Boys dorm father, nudged Eddie's shoulder. 'I'm fine right here,' Eddie said, his voice cracking.

'Come here,' Silvera said.

He got up grudgingly and struggled past chairs and legs until he was standing in front of Silvera.

'What do you want?' Eddie asked, but it sounded more like a threat than a question.

Silvera pointed at the stool. 'This is your seat.'

'What do you want?'

Silvera lunged forward and Eddie hurried to the stool. He

sat with his back hunched. He stared at the floor.

'Spit it out, Eddie.'

'I don't know what you're talking about.'

'I hear you've got a problem getting it up.'

A murmur rippled through the room.

'Quiet!' Silvera shouted. 'All of you, you're here at my invitation. Keep quiet!'

'What do you want from me?' Eddie said. He looked frightened. He looked guilty. But of what? And how could a person look guilty when you don't even know what they've been accused of?

'Why did you do it?' Silvera said, with syrupy, mocking concern.

Eddie shook his head and stared blankly at the man. Finally he said: 'I was horny.'

'Why trick girls into sleeping with you?' Silvera asked. 'Couldn't you find a girlfriend? Couldn't you wait for homegoing?'

Eddie shook his head.

'Answer me.'

'No.'

'Why not?'

'I don't know.'

'You don't know?'

Eddie shook his head.

'Okay,' Silvera said loudly. 'Fine. Call when you figure it out. You're expelled, too. *Now. Out.*'

Eddie slipped off the stool and hurried out of the dining room. But before he left, just as he was through the door, he turned and said, 'You only wish you could get some too!' He rushed out and the heavy door slammed shut behind him.

I felt dizzy from the heat, from anger. Oh, was I angry! Whatever Eddie was, whatever Patrick and I were, Silvera was even worse. The man was sick, crazy, an evangelist gone mad, a Stalinist agent with hemorrhoids!

Silvera paced. His shirt was wet down the back and under

the arms. He ran his hands through his black hair so many times it was slicked down.

'Sex,' he said, 'will ruin you! Sex ruins relationships. You cannot be friends and have sex. Sex outside of marriage atrophies love.' He clapped his hands together. 'All right. What's going on here? What is the issue here? I'll tell you what the issue is. The issue is deceit.'

I looked at Louise. She, too, had been accused of the mysterious something. I expected to see a reflection of my own mute anger in her face, an identical reaction, but it wasn't there. Her face showed fear and shame. She was completely still.

'Eddie has used my name,' Silvera said, 'for sexual credit. He has connived and deceived and yes he has received sex on the basis of forged letters from me granting him permission to explore his blocked libido. What shocks me is that anyone would believe him. How could any halfway intelligent person believe such a cheap charade? I'll tell you how: because they wanted to. It is not a matter of simple coercion, it is also a matter of volunteerism.'

He paused as Louise stood up. His eyes burned into her as she navigated the crowded room. As she neared the door, Silvera called her name. She stopped, but did not answer.

'Don't go, Louise,' he said. 'We need you, Louise. If you go, you'll be abandoning yourself.'

Her back expanded slightly, as if she were taking a long, deep breath, and she walked slowly and steadily toward the door. Jimmy ran after her.

Silvera laughed. He rolled his eyes and smiled. 'You know?' he said — the faker, the liar — 'I have to doubt a love that allows one party to betray the other one so freely.' His laugh was hollow, tinny. 'Louise had agreed to *help* Eddie. Isn't that funny?'

No one laughed.

He turned to me again. My whole body stiffened in my chair. I wouldn't move; he couldn't move me. He said, 'And here's our resident virgin.'

Who told him that? How was it his business? Why was he telling the whole school?

He shook his head. 'Dear little Kate. Angel of addiction. Saint of purity. Girl in the black negligée.'

'Wait a minute!' I said. 'What are you talking about?'

'You knew,' Silvera said, 'that Patrick was covering up for Eddie in return for a supply of drugs. He typed the letters and you delivered them. And you lied about yourself to your friends.'

'I didn't!' I said.

I looked at the faces surrounding me for support and understanding. These were the people with whom I lived, shared air and food, slept, joked. Yet I couldn't read them. Silvera's words, the wildness of his claims, was pulling me outside of their circle of trust.

'Don't lie to us, Kate,' he said softly, with conviction.

'No!' I shouted. 'You're *wrong*. I didn't do any of that! I've never lied! Ted,' I pleaded, 'tell him.'

Ted shrugged meekly.

I looked at Gwen and demanded, 'Tell him!'

She looked at me stony-faced. Her eyes were welling with tears, but she wouldn't speak on my behalf. She knew, if anyone did, that I knew nothing about Eddie or his arrangements with Patrick, and that I had never been to bed with a boy in my life. But then, yes, she had slipped the negligée back into my suitcase. And I remembered, now like a confession, her words of the night before: 'I'm sorry,' she had said.

The rest was a blur of voices and faces that culminated in a sensation of peacefulness. Maybe I fainted, I don't know. All I remember is waking up in middle of the night and seeing Gwen asleep in her bed, huddled under her blanket. When I sat up and my covers fell off, I found I was still dressed. It was four-thirty in the morning. In a couple of hours, the machine of Grove would begin its grind.

I had only one thought: to leave, escape, steal my butterfly wings and claim freedom.

# EIGHT

Running away. Actually, I was walking. Walking and thinking and feeling cold and excited about the power of walking away. Of making my own decision not to play the Grove games. It was one thing to go along with the flow, to exist in a moderate state between privacy and Grove theory, as I felt I had managed before. But it was another thing to be grease for the wheels of the machine. How that had come about deeply confused me. Pieces of information glued themselves together in my mind with speculation. *When, where, who, why, how?* For an instant, less than a second, as I was waiting at the light across the street from the deserted mall (waiting for a red light to turn green on an empty street, deep in the night, with no one around to see: playing straight by the rules), I experienced a wave of belief in Silvera's story. *The girl in the black negligée. Angel of addiction.* Then, just as suddenly, my momentary insanity ended and I knew, definitely, that I was innocent. I had done nothing but wear the negligée. I had done nothing but trust Patrick. I knew exactly where I stood in relation to the truth. But that was all I knew about: myself. I was alone now. I didn't know about anyone else.

I called a taxi from a pay phone. As I waited, I argued with myself over calling Patrick when I got home. Silvera was a powerful man, and he had created in me an edge of distrust. I tried to fight it, but it was there: questions with no answers, doubts borne of accusations. Patrick had seemed fine to me — healthy, happy — since returning to school and starting Drug Group. Yet, probably because he had deceived me once before, I found myself capable of believing that he had continued to mask his addiction. I couldn't forget how he had lied to me about the letters; he had to have had a reason, something more compelling than his love for me. I vascillated between an intense, unconditional love, and suspicion of betrayal. One minute I was impatient to get home and call him, and the next, I promised myself I never would.

The taxi finally came and I got in. 'Bus station,' I said.
'Which one?'
The driver's bloodshot eyes in the rearview mirror frightened me. I didn't know which one, but I couldn't let him know I was lost.
'Bus to New York,' I said.
He let me off in front of a Greyhound station in a narrow side street. The door was locked so I waited outside. After about an hour, the sky started to get light, and then at last the sun rose: peachy streaks in the grey sky, then vivid blue. An attendant came around and opened the door. He told me that the first bus to the city was in twenty minutes. That was a relief; it was still too early for Grove to miss me. By the time they realized I was gone, I would have been on the bus for over an hour.

It was noon but felt like days later when I finally reached home. I opened the door with my key. The phone was ringing. Mom, of course, would be at the office. I started to run to answer it, but realized it could have been someone from Grove, so didn't. By that time they would have been looking for me; they would have been at the inform-the-parents stage. The dining room would be packed for lunch and the word would be out that Kate had run away. Maybe

Silvera was telling them Patrick and I had plotted it and left together. Maybe that wouldn't have been such a bad idea.

I went up to my room and slept. When I woke up, Betty was curled between my feet, and I felt comforted. Everything was so much clearer. It now seemed to me that if Silvera had lied about me not being a virgin, he could have lied about Patrick being back on drugs. Not to mention Louise sleeping with Eddie. Or was there some truth to Silvera's lies? Maybe, at least, he really believed them . . . or had been led to believe them. *By Gwen*. But why had she done it?

Betty followed me downstairs. I made myself a sandwich, and was eating it at the kitchen table when the front door creaked open. Mom appeared in the kitchen, wearing a stylish brown suit and a white silk blouse with a fluffy bow at the neck. She wore large pearl earrings and deep red lipstick. She stood there looking at me before taking a slow breath and sitting down.

'Hi Mom,' I said, my mouth full of tuna fish.

'Hello dear,' she said softly.

'What's up?'

'Funny, I was going to ask you the same.'

'I guess they called you,' I said.

She sighed. 'Is there any more of that tuna fish? I'm starved.'

I made her a sandwich. She ate the first half before speaking again.

'Gene Silvera called me,' she said.

'What did he tell you?'

'That there had been quite a bit of confusion about a boy —'

'Eddie?'

'Yes. And another one — '

'Patrick didn't do anything!'

Mom was silent for a moment, then she said, 'Mr Silvera explained that there had been some misapprehension concerning Eddie, and that it's been cleared up — '

'How? Did he tell you how?'

'No, sweetheart, not exactly. But he assured me there would be no problem with your returning to school. He understands that you were quite upset.'

'How can you believe that pig!'

'Kate! He is an intelligent man with excellent credentials! Your father and I put our trust in him when we chose the school for you!'

I shook my head. 'I am not going back to that place!'

'Kate, darling, you have to go back.'

'But I can't, Mom.'

I tried to explain my thoughts of that morning, but it came out garbled and confused. She watched me with what appeared to be a mixture of sympathy and disbelief. She could not bring herself to believe Gwen had had anything to do with it. She was convinced I was exaggerating, that I was emotionally distraught over Patrick, that any misinterpretation of my conduct could be cleared up. She was convinced that Silvera was 'a responsible, rational man.'

'Please,' I begged. 'Let me stay home. *Please*.'

'Dear,' she said, shaking her head sadly. 'I can't walk away from my life either. You have to face this.'

'Just let me stay home!'

'You don't understand. I'm selling the house. It's on the market and already someone's shown interest. My plans are to move into the city to be closer to the office, though I won't look for my own place until the house is sold. I'll rent. The divorce is going through, sweetheart, it's happening. Dad and I agreed that I won't ask for alimony, and he'll let me buy out his half of the business for one dollar.'

'One dollar?'

She nodded.

No wonder Dad had looked so ragged and poor over Thanksgiving.

'He has a new office. Well, it isn't *new*. It's a little run down, but he'll grow out of it in no time.' She leaned forward and touched my arm. Looking gravely into my eyes, the way mothers do when they want you to know they're serious, she said, 'It's better this way. We both want everything completely separate.'

'What about me?'

'Well, we both get a hundred percent of you.' She smiled.

'How?' I said. 'I'm one person, you can't split me down the middle.'

'We'll share you.' That smile. 'You have to go back to school, Kate. That's just the way it is.'

I was full of fight, of determination to win my case, but as I sat there searching for a new angle by which to convince her, her troubled face convinced me instead. She had just come right out and told me that we had no house now. There was no more *we* and no more mutual home. Home now was wherever each of us happened to be. Their divorce had disowned me from their protection. If I ran, I would have to run in circles. There was nowhere to go.

We drove back to Grove in silence. I was sick at the thought of returning to that place, and sicker that it was Mom who was taking me back. I tried to understand why she was doing it, but I couldn't help blaming her. I kept thinking that she hated me and was abandoning me to a distorted life of lies and misinterpretation. It was no use trying to explain. Home was over.

And so, less than twenty-four hours after leaving Grove, I returned. I had walked away and had been run right back. Patrick was gone. Gwen had betrayed me. Mom didn't want me. That was how I felt and I could see no reason to sustain an illusion that things would improve. Every connection to love had been snapped. I lay on my bed with my hands folded over my stomach and decided never to move again. I would just lie there until I died.

A vague light strayed in from the lamp on the path outside, and silvery silhouettes emerged on the objects in the room. The longer I stared, the brighter the outlines became, until the room seemed strung with a network of silver hairs. It was magical. Time stopped and space reformed. I was not in my room at Grove, but in a compartment of darkness within a cloisonné of light.

I could be a metaphysicist, I thought, if I lived.

Then the door burst open and a block of light from the hallway fell across the floor. Gwen barrelled in.

'Don't turn on the light,' I said. 'I'm going to sleep.' And I meant: for good.

'Kate! I am *so* glad to see you!' She bounded onto my bed and tried to wrestle a hug out of me.

I said, 'Stop it!' and she pulled back.

Her eyes flitted across my face. 'What's wrong?' she asked.

Didn't she know? Didn't she understand that her betrayal had severed our friendship?

'Never mind,' I said. 'It doesn't matter anymore.'

'What the fuck do you mean, it doesn't matter anymore? Will you at least listen to me? I had to do it. I *had* to. I didn't have any choice.'

I rolled over and faced the window. Kids were heading down for study hall.

'Okay,' she said, standing abruptly. She shut the door with a bang and it was dark again. She stood in the middle of the room and stamped her foot twice to get my attention. 'I never went to New Jersey for Thanksgiving.'

I closed my eyes. 'I couldn't care less.'

'I had an abortion in New York. Kate, are you listening? Listen.'

My stomach lurched. An abortion? But what did that have to do with Eddie, or me, or Patrick, or any of this? I squeezed my eyes tighter.

'I'm telling you the truth,' she said, 'so listen.'

'Liar.'

'No. I am telling you the *truth*. I couldn't before, Kate, no one knows the truth about me.'

'Great, and everyone knows lies about me.'

'Eddie gave me the money for the abortion.'

Nothing was clear. 'You mean you slept with Eddie?'

'No way! It was a guy last summer, late August, just one of those things. But I knew Eddie had money. He was selling dope to Patrick, Kate — *listen* — that's just the fact. Maybe not recently, but before. That's how Patrick got his stuff. And Patrick was covering for Eddie. Eddie told me himself.'

'You believe him?'

'Maybe not. I don't know. But the deal was he'd give me the money if I would sleep with him. I said sure, okay, but you have to wait two weeks after an abortion to heal. We made a date. I got back to school the other day and I couldn't do it. I knew all this weird stuff was happening with Eddie. I wanted to nark on him. I wanted to get him into some more trouble so he'd forget about sleeping with me. Not that I was ever going to sleep with him, I'd *never* do it with Eddie! He's such a sleaze. I told him about the party and he typed up his name a couple of times and I tossed the slips in the box. I swear, I was just as surprised Lee Lee did it too, for Laura. I knew about those letters from you, and kind of figured the rest out. It was really just a wild guess. After the party, I went to Silvera and told him about Patrick and Eddie and I said Eddie was onto a whole bunch of girls. Silvera ate it up. So I thought, well, if I just add a little fat to the fire, Eddie will be expelled. The next thing I knew, Pam pulled me into her room and started asking me questions about you and Patrick. It was like they were trying to count up all the rules he ever broke. I didn't mean it to go that way, Kate, I really want you to believe me. Eddie must have told them Patrick was still taking dope. I know he wasn't. Jesus, everyone in Drug Group knows that.'

'I know that too.'

'I had to keep the questions away from myself. So I told her I didn't know about you two, that for all I knew you were sleeping together, but I couldn't vouch for it. I told her you borrowed my black negligée because Patrick was coming home with you for Thanksgiving.'

'Asshole!'

'Good, let it out. Get mad at me. I deserve it.'
'Give me a break, Gwen.'
'I didn't know Silvera was going to say what he said. I swear, I would have warned you. I figured he'd say something about Patrick, that was all.'
'That was more than enough.'
'I'm sorry. I'm really sorry.'
'So now you've gotten fifteen million people expelled and no one knows you had an abortion.'
'Just you.'
'Why did you tell me? What makes you think you can trust me?'
'Can't I?'
'Not necessarily.' I sat up. 'In fact, maybe I'll just go tell Silvera all about it. Maybe I'll do what you did and fuck things up for you so I can get Patrick back into school.'
'They'll never believe you,' she said. Then she smiled and sat on my bed. 'Besides, he's already back in. He talked to Silvera and proved he hasn't been using drugs. He never even left campus.'
'He's *here*?'
'Yup.'
'Does he know I'm back?'
'I don't know. Maybe. I didn't know you were back.'
I sat on the edge of my bed next to Gwen. I didn't know if I believed her story or, if it was really true, if I'd be able to forgive her. I couldn't help feeling hurt.
'Hit me,' she said. 'Go on, do it.'
I shook my head. I didn't even have the emotional energy left to curse her out.
'Promise you'll do something really mean to me later?'
I shrugged. 'Maybe.' Then I smiled, just a touch of forgiveness, and said, 'If you're good.'
Patrick had heard I was back. I went to the lobby windows and saw him standing in front of Girls Dorm with that incredible patience of his, that slow sexy *waiting* of which he was a master. I felt as if I were waking up from a nightmare.

Yet a nightmare, real or not, leaves behind a bitterness, a telltale exhaustion. I felt half-relieved and half-unbelieving, half-deceived by half-truths. My reality was shifting to include illusion, deception, lies. Who was Patrick, and why did he love me — and did he love me? — and was he really standing out there waiting for me? If I went downstairs, swallowed up by the stairwell in the process, would he be there when I arrived or would he, *poof,* be gone?

He waved. He said something that exuded a cloud of frozen breath, but I couldn't understand. He motioned for me to come outside. *Come, come, I'm waiting.* As I walked down the stairs, I prepared myself for him not to be there when I arrived.

But he was.

He smiled and laughed when he saw me. 'Okay?' he said, reaching out his arms.

I shook my head. 'I'm not going to study hall,' I told him.

'You don't have to. Silvera gave us permission to stay up here together. I didn't even ask. He told me you were back.'

'Permission? But you kneed him.'

'I panicked. He understands. I spent hours talking my way back in last night. He knows I've been straight, he believes me. I'm not messing my life up again, Kate. I really meant what I said in the meeting, that I don't have anywhere else to go.'

'Neither do I, that's what I found out today.'

He lay his hand gently on my waist. 'None of this should have happened,' he said. 'Did you talk to Gwen?'

I told him I had.

'She was mysterious about it,' he said. 'But all day she kept saying she'd be able to explain.'

'She didn't tell you?'

He shook his head.

'Maybe I'll tell you later,' I said. I was tempted to betray her, to advertise what she'd worked so hard at hiding. But I wasn't sure. We could all go on betraying each other and the pain would never end. It had to stop somewhere and I knew if I wanted, it could stop with me.

'So,' he smiled, 'I heard about what Silvera said about you.'

'Oh *God*.'

'No one ever believed it, anyway.'

'Patrick? Why did you do that for Eddie, with the letters? Why did you lie to me — '

'I didn't mean to lie. He lied to *me*. He said they were jokes, you know, anonymous love letters, just to get the girls excited. I never read them.'

'The fat man said you typed them.'

'Eddie typed them. I just said I'd ask you to get them to the girls.'

'Why didn't you tell me they were jokes? If that was all you thought, I mean.'

'Eddie said not to. He said you'd just tell the girls.'

'But what about Louise? Didn't you wonder — '

'Kate, I swear, I thought she'd laugh it off. I didn't know.'

# PART TWO

# NINE

In the beginning, the excitement of Patrick touching my arm, looking at me googily-eyed, kissing me impulsively, was all that mattered. But love gets wise. Three months, though not a long time, was long enough to understand what he had said when he first got expelled from school. In answer to my courageous assertion of love — saying the words — he had turned before stepping into the cab and said, 'That's not the point anymore.'

And that wasn't the point anymore.

Shades of doubt and anger had blended with the innocence of our love for each other. It wasn't just a matter of passing time and building experience, it was the drugs. Using or not, he was an addict. As with an alcoholic, stopping use of the drug did not cure the disease. The disease was the desire for heroin, the physical knowledge of how good it felt, the craving, the crazy release. Addiction was a yearning stronger than love. You could look at another girl, or into a bottle, or through the eye of a needle and feel the same thing: an insane chemical lust. *Using* as an addict — using sex or wine or smack — is like chaining yourself to the heavens: all you have is that brief moment of freedom, that instant release, and then you're shackled again to the observation of life from the cloudy distance of your pain. Some heaven! I yearned for freedom too, but looked for it in Patrick. He was my addiction; I needed him to need me, and believed that with my support he could become healthy and free. I was wrong about that, of course; addicts can only be freed by themselves. But I didn't know that then, I was totally ensconced in him and in us; and so, in a way, his addiction controlled me, too. It was a hopeless fight which I was determined to win. I came to think of my foe — his addiction — as another girl, a seductive force with the power to pull him away. When he craved *her,* his imagination wandered away from me. When I suspected he was starting to drift, when I sensed it or saw it in his eyes, I became jealous. Jealous of *her,* of the drug, of his desire to be released from his body to heaven. To be released from me, because I tended to bind him to reality, which was, for him, a hell.

We were getting to know each other, there was no way around it. We spent December always close, but two steps back, scrutinizing each other's faces and words and silences. Finally, we formalized our exploration of each other into a kind of game.

It was an idea conceived in a moment of frustration. Silvera's value judgements — *angel of addiction, girl in the black negligée* – irked me. I would lead Patrick in ridicule of the man, the fat man, frog king, monster blob, hypocrite, liar, fag. We were cruel. It was great. But sometimes Patrick would resist. It was on one such occasion, as we were walking up the icy hill after dinner, that he told me to 'drop it.'

'What do you mean?' I asked, hurt by his sudden withdrawal from comraderie.

He stared at me from within the cave of his army jacket hood. 'Just forget it,' he said.

'What? Forget *what*?' He started up the hill and I followed. 'Forget what you just said? or forget that I'm trapped here?'

'Trapped?' he said. 'If you're trapped, you've done it to yourself.'

That stung. 'If that's what you think, then why do you hang out with me?'

'If *what's* what I think?'

'That I'm making myself unhappy. I mean, doesn't it occur to you that you're making me unhappy, too?'

'You don't have to stay with me,' he said. 'I've got problems of my own. I can't be responsible for your unhappiness, too.'

'Too? I didn't know you were so unhappy, you never expressed that to me.'

People were struggling past us on the narrow, semi-shovelled path, so we moved off to the side and stood ankle-deep in snow. And that was how it started: standing in the snow, facing each other, venting steam. After that, it became a planned ritual, a kind of joint therapy that we engaged in for about fifteen minutes almost every day between dinner and study hall.

We would go down to the snowy field behind the science building, and stand like two ice people, frozen still, facing each other. We made some rules: no touching (we did enough of that the rest of the time); no blaming; don't default to love-related excuses like *I did it because I love you* or *it doesn't really matter anyway because I love you*; be honest.

Snow flurried down, white specks flickering in the twilit darkness, drifting to earth. The science field was an expanse of untouched whiteness, like a blank sheet stretched flat on a windless day. Patrick stood straight as a pole an arm's length in front of me, just too far to reach. His hood was gathered around his face, leaving only a small hole through which his eyes, nose and mouth were visible. He looked like a baby, all bundled up. Frozen clouds misted the air as we spoke.

He said, 'Last night I dreamed I got up in the middle of the night and snuck into your dorm. I was looking for you, but couldn't find your room and went into someone else's room by mistake. I got into someone's bed knowing it wasn't yours. Then the girl in the bed rolled over and it was you.'

'Very interesting,' I said, thinking he had seen *her*, my foe, in his own dream. 'Tell me more.'

'She was wearing pink.'

'Did she have breasts?'

'Two.'

'But were they big?'

'Average, I think.'

'What color was her hair?'

'She didn't have any hair. That was the strange thing.'

'Do you resent me because we haven't slept together?'

'I don't know. I guess so.'

'All this virgin stuff — I'm almost sixteen.'

He paused. 'But to be honest, Kate, I don't want to marry you.'

'No one asked you to.'

'I asked you. Remember?'

Lying next to each other in sleeping bags. The girl in the black negligée. I nodded.

'You don't care for me enough to make a commitment, I said. Theoretically, far in the future, I mean. But you desire my body?'

'That's not it. It's just that I don't know who I am.'

'I know who you are.'

'How can you? If *I* don't know who I am, then you can't know.'

'What about me? Do you know who I am?'

'Kate Steiner. My favorite girlfriend.'

'Favorite?'

'Only.'

'Now.'

'Are you jealous of past loves?'

'I thought you told me you didn't love any of them.'

'Not really. Not like you.'

'I resent that.'

'What? That I had girlfriends before you? Big deal. It's only normal. I mean, I'm a man.'

'Boy.'

'Male.'

'I don't like being compared. I hate being compared. Even if you say to me that I'm pretty, so much prettier than other girls you've known, or that you love me more, it's no good because just bringing them up is a kind of betrayal.'

'Bullshit, Kate.'

'That's what I think.'

'That's what *you* think.'

'Thanks a lot for the consideration. What I really want to say is that I think it's self-centered. You can be self-centered.'

'What else can I be? Should *you* be my center?'

'You could think about how I would feel when you make fun of something I say, or stop listening because you're tired of it.'

'Is that what I do? Why are you throwing that at me now? Why haven't you ever said it before?'

'Because it hasn't come to mind.'

'Then it isn't so important to you.'

'Yes it is. Don't think you can tell me what I think just because you're a man.'

'Boy.' He smiled. 'Besides, I don't do that.'

'You put words into my mouth by dreaming about me,' I said. 'You build up expectations when you dream about me.'

'You don't dream about me?'

'Sometimes.'

'Maybe it isn't building up expectations, maybe it's expressing desires. I *do* desire to sleep with you. I want to make love to the girl of my dreams.'

I thought about it. Who doesn't want that? In my dreams of Patrick — and I never told him about them — I saw *her*, my rival. She was pretty, with a short black pageboy haircut, lily white skin and cherry red lips. She was taller than me and about the same weight, but more voluptuously built, with a tight little waist fanning up into boobs and down into hips. She was a sexy girl, and she attracted him. He would go to her. Sometimes he would leave me altogether and sometimes he would keep her secretly. Either way, I would go looking for him and find her instead. She would tell me he had made his choice. I would tell her he had chosen wrongly. She would laugh at me as if I were naive, foolishly innocent. In the end, Patrick would return to me and promise his devotion. I would always wake up from these dreams feeling disturbed and convinced that, in time, he would leave me. In my dream he would return, but in real life, when it happened, he wouldn't.

It was on the sixteenth of December, in the afternoon, that I decided to give him his dream so that I might have mine. I told him in the snow later that day. I said, 'Okay, let's do it. Make love to me for real.'

'Are you sure?'

'I've thought about it. Yes, I'm positive.'

We set the date for New Year's Eve.

All we had to do was pass our midterm exams, before winter vacation. If you failed, you had to stay at school over the two-week vacation and take the exams again. We would have to study hard.

Gwen promised to help us. She was as meticulous in her day-to-day studies as she was in making sharp hospital corners on her bed. Because of her messy verbal onslaughts, people assumed she was an all-round slob. But Gwen had her world carefully worked out; she knew where everything was, from socks to information. Her perfect order and the aggression with which she pursued it was no mystery to me; I had been her pawn. She was still trying to make amends for that, which was why she offered to tutor us. She even threw in a guarantee that we would pass all our exams with at least a B.

'Kate! When did the French Revolution start?'

'Patrick! What forms the compound of nitric acid?'

'Does anyone know why Madame Bovary wasn't content to stay home?'

'If three kids go to the store to buy seventeen loaves of bread and one kid has fifty-three cents, another has twenty-four cents and the third has seventy-five cents, how much does each loaf of bread cost if all totalled they end up with just a nickel between them?'

She also took over the daily cleaning of our room *and* the big Saturday cleanup. She was determined to win me back. But I didn't feel I could trust her. She cleaned well and was a solid tutor, and I appreciated those things (who wouldn't?), but she had put a big dent in our friendship and couldn't just bang it out instantly with favors.

Mom was living in Manhattan with a roommate — another woman — and she had already invited Gwen for vacation. I was uneasy about letting her deeper into what I had left of a family. The Eddie incident still confused me. I could understand Gwen's motives: the abortion must have been horrible, and to have gone through it all alone! But it frightened me to realize how fiercely self-protective she could be. How low would she stoop again, if circumstances dictated? Or had she learned something about the value of friendship? Could she, if I didn't give her another chance? I couldn't decide whether or not to let her come home with me; and when the subject came up, I wasn't prepared.

One morning, as she moved efficiently across the floor with a broom, she stopped at my bed — where I was slowly waking up — and said, 'Am I supposed to get a present for your mother's roommate, or what?'

I sat up on the edge of the bed and tapped my feet on the floor in search of my slippers. Gwen broomed them over to me. I slipped my feet in and stood. She handed me my bathrobe.

She said, 'So? Should I?'

'I don't know, Gwen,' I said, and it must have sounded as uncommitted as I felt, because her face froze. Gwen was a wizard at reading between the lines — and using her understanding to get her way. She pinned her eyes right on me, teasing out guilt by the pound.

'I'm sorry,' I said. 'I just — '

'Forget it.' She grabbed her yellow jacket and dashed out of the room.

She didn't mention it at all that day. But later that night, between curfew and lights out, she retaliated. It was inevitable; Gwen did not let things pass.

I was sitting on my bed, alone in the room, reviewing material from English Lit. There was a soft knock on the door and then four tiny brown fingers curled around the edge. A bright white sneaker toed its way in, followed by the leg, torso, shoulder, then face of Rawlene. She was wearing her fluffy blue bathrobe. Her ironed hair was molded into a reverse flip in the back, and her bangs curved up like a stiff gutter pipe. Her robe was slightly open at the bottom and I saw her red Be Here Butterfly dress with the black sequin trim.

'You're invited to a show tonight,' she said. 'Come on out, the BHBs wait for no woman.'

It wasn't unusual for the BHBs to make surprise appearances — anywhere, anytime — so I followed her down the hall to the lobby.

A few girls sat around talking or reading. There was no sign of a show.

'Wait right here,' Rawlene said, and disappeared down the other hall way.

I sat in one of two beat-up vinyl chairs — one was pea green, and the other was Golden's mustard yellow — and waited. A record scratched, and then guitars, pianos and drums harmonized into the Osmond Bros. There was a confusion of footsteps and then out they came: Rawlene, Nicole, Amy — and then Gwen. She wore the famous (or infamous) black negligée and stood in front of the Be Here Butterflies, swaying her hips to their rhythm and slowly opening her arms. Gwen handled the synchronized dance steps pretty well, and I was impressed. But it was *funny*. She had the steps, not the style. Even the BHBs barely had style, but at least they had potential.

Rawlene suddenly shouted, 'Yo!' and the music snapped off.

The Be Here's plus Gwen swayed to silence. Gwen fell back into the ranks. They all dragged one arm to the right, and the other arm to the left, so they were standing with their open arms crisscrossing each other's. Then they started to hum and Gwen stepped forward. They sang:

Gwen: 'One bad apple don't spoil the whole bunch a girls, *oooh,* gimme one more chance — '

Amy: 'Gimme!'

Nicole: 'Gimme!'

Rawlene: 'Gimme!'

They all took four tiny steps to the left, then four tiny steps to the right, clapped their hands twice and spun around. They came to a jolting halt with their legs spread apart. They threw their arms into Vs and raised their faces toward the ceiling.

I burst out laughing; it was just too weird.

Then, to my horror, Gwen lunged to her knee in my direction. The BHB's fell out of formation.

Amy said, 'Give it up, Kate. It's time to forgive your sister!'

'That's right,' said Nicole. 'Gwen's *askin'* you.'

Gwen was staring at me with the persistent, big-eyed face of a poster waif. I couldn't believe it; I was being bamboozled, guilted into befriending her, refriending her. Not that we'd ever really stopped being friends, just absolute *best* friends. I could feel my resistance bending. Voices of the Be Here Butterflies echoed: 'Sisters . . . fuckin' Silvera . . . gotta understand . . . Superfly justice . . . gotta stand by your sisters . . . gotta gotta . . . do right . . . *yo.*'

Finally I said, 'Okay, come home with me if that's what you want, Gwen.' Home was relative now, anyway. As was friendship. As was love.

The room broke into applause. Gwen sprang up clapping.

She got that old cocky look on her face — eyebrows arching, a wide grin — and then she asked me, 'So, should I get a gift for your mother's roommate, or what?'

On the second day of midterms there was a storm: the sky turned pale green, snow flickered down like chips of granite. In the end, everything was white. Trees were crystal webs. Trails of footsteps mapped the school's life.

Patrick and I studied so hard and were so sure we'd pass our exams, that we celebrated in advance. After study hall one night, we ran through the shimmering snow to the science field. The sky was pitch black, starless, and the snow covering the field was pure bleached heaven. We rolled snowballs into boulders and erected a snowman. Patrick gave him a cigarette and I gave him my blue and red striped scarf.

'Reverend White,' Patrick addressed the snowman. 'Will you kindly marry us?'

I laughed. 'But you don't want to marry me, remember?'

Smiling, he shook his head. 'It was a lie.'

I slapped him playfully. He caught my arm and pulled me to him. 'Well, do you want to?'

'For real?'

'Right now.'

So we stood in front of the Reverend White, who glowed silvery round under the dark sky. Patrick looked at me and very gently said, 'I, Patrick Nevins, promise to love and adore, hold and protect you, Kate, for the rest of my life.'

I looked into Patrick's eyes: deep blue, intense. 'I, Kate Steiner, promise to love and adore, hold and protect you, Patrick, for the rest of my life.'

'I have no ring,' he said.

'We have no home,' I said.

He took my hand and squeezed it. Warmth filled me on that freezing night. A wind rushed over us and then the air settled into a complete calm.

On the morning of December twenty-third, the test results were posted in the first floor of the school building. After breakfast everyone poured into the hallway and crowded in front of the board. Happy voices erupted and a few long-faced kids walked silently away.

Patrick and I darted around, searching out our scores. My heart pounded as I read one pass after another. Seven passes! I had made it! I spun around looking for Patrick. He was sitting on the stairs, elbows propped on knees, staring into clasped hands. His lips were drawn in, buttoned up, defeated.

'Patrick?' I said softly.

He shook his head.

There were two one-week sessions during vacation, two more chances to pass midterms. 'You'll pass in the first session,' I said. 'I'm sure you will.'

He said, 'I'll try,' but he sounded uncertain.

The buses left for the city that afternoon. I tried to cheer him up, but it was impossible. He was settled into the gloomy surprise of having failed, of having to stay behind. The one note of optimism was his determination to see me on New Year's Eve. He kept saying, 'I'll be there, don't worry, I'll definitely be there.' I hoped he *would* be there, but it was scary to really expect him. I was afraid that our New Year's plans would turn out to be nothing but a fantasy. Patrick was determined, though. He said, 'We consummate our marriage on New Year's Eve.'

It was awful saying goodbye to him in front of the buses, watching him walk back up toward the dorms, vanishing into Grove as I prepared to leave. I was so worried about him! Why hadn't I failed something too, just to stay behind and help him? But it was too late; I was on one list, and he was on another.

He was still moving up the hill when I was herded onto the bus with Gwen.

# TEN

'Lookit,' Gwen said, as we lugged our suitcases through the crazed holiday crowd at the Port Authority bus terminal. 'All I'm saying is a little makeup never hurt anyone.'

'I'm just not that kind of person.'

'What do you mean *that kind of person?* What am I, some kind of cheap date? Jesus F. Christ, I get knocked up once,' she shouted, 'and you act like I'm some kind of street walker!'

People were staring at us. I walked fast, pretending not to know her.

'Kate!' She chased me. 'Kate!'

Finally I said, 'You could be a little more discreet!'

'Ha!' she said — 'Ha!' — but she didn't sound amused. 'Discreet? But I have a pale complexion, Kate. Did you hear me? Mrs Nevins! My complexion is too pale!'

I dashed through the door to the taxi stand outside, trying to get away before Gwen caught up with me. I had told her not to call me Mrs Nevins. Sharing the experience with her had been a mistake. I should have known better. All information — secrets or not — ultimately became Gwen's property. At least I hadn't told her about my plans for New Year's Eve.

'Okay,' Gwen said, racing up behind me. 'I apologize.'
I didn't answer, didn't even look at her.
'You're being too hard on me. Give me a break, okay? *Okay?*'

A cab drove up, and a man in a grey suit and camelhair coat tried to cut in front of us. Gwen pushed past him, saying, 'Come on, Kate, get in!'

'Where to?' the cabbie asked.

'Where to?' Gwen repeated to me.

I pulled the slip of paper from my jacket pocket. '989 Park Avenue.'

'What cross street?' he asked.

Gwen and I looked at each other. I shrugged. She said, '989 Park Avenue. What are you, deaf?'

989 Park Avenue — Mom's swanky new address — put Dad's crosstown digs to shame. It was a huge old limestone building with a blue awning perched on brass poles. When a man in a navy blue uniform rushed out and took our bags, I thought he was trying to rob us.

'Don't be a dufus,' Gwen said. 'He's the doorman!'

Ah, yes — the doorman. Growing up in the suburbs, then sequestered at Grove, I had never encountered this urban species. Not even at Dad's; his building was strictly self-serve elevator.

'I'm John,' the doorman said. 'Mrs Steiner said to expect you.' He smiled, more at us than with us. It was like we were a couple of hicks. I guess we were.

Gwen, *sophisticate extraordinaire,* didn't like it. She said, 'Please show us to the elevator,' and marched into the building.

The large foyer had a polished marble floor and was furnished with four couches, two armchairs and a huge glass vase filled with orange tiger lilies and sprigs of eucalyptus. A sparkling chandelier hung from the middle of the ceiling. John deposited us with our suitcases in front of a polished brass elevator at the far end of the foyer.

We rode up to the eleventh floor. I looked at the paper. '11D,' I said. And Gwen rang the bell.

A tall woman with short grey hair answered. She wiped her hands on a striped canvas apron — which she wore over white slacks and a black cashmere turtleneck — before offering to shake.

'I'm Ann,' she said, flashing a smile, 'your Mom's roommate. She just phoned to say she'll be a little late from the office. Come on in.'

The apartment was big and homey, cluttered with antiques, abstract prints, books, piles of unopened mail, and filled with good, spicy smells.

'I was just cooking,' Ann said. 'Your room's the one next to the bathroom. Make yourselves comfortable. I'll be in the kitchen.'

We wandered through a large living room with a Persian rug and long blue couch, which Gwen promptly tested. 'It's filled with feathers!' she said, sinking back. An adjacent dining room was dominated by a huge round table surrounded by carved antique chairs. The walls were forest green. 'What a place!' Gwen said, trailing me. Our bedroom was sparse and tiny: formerly the maid's room, now crammed with twin beds, a tall dresser, and a fancy gumball machine filled with multicolored candies. I twisted the knob but nothing came out. We left our suitcases on the beds and went exploring. There were two more bedrooms — Mom's and Ann's — and a small study. It was lined with bookshelves, and in the center of the room was an antique partners' desk. There, on a worn green blotter, was Betty, sitting like a prim feline statue. She looked at me and yawned.

'Hey, little Betty!' I scooped her into a hug from which she extricated herself with a war cry. She skidded out of the room.

'She's her same old charming self,' Gwen said. 'Come on, let's follow that smell.'

We found the kitchen just beyond the foyer. There was a

square table-for-two tucked in a corner. We sat there, dipping carrot sticks into sour cream, and talking to Ann as she cooked. She said that a 'special friend' of Mom's was due for dinner.

'Who?' I asked.

'I don't think you know him.'

Gwen mouthed *him* and raised her eyebrows.

I crunched loudly on a carrot stick.

'I hope you like steak *au poivre*,' Ann said.

'Steak-o-what?' Gwen asked.

'Steak with pepper. It's good.'

'I'll try anything once,' Gwen said. 'Are you a chef?'

Ann pounded medallions of steak with a wooden mallet. 'Just amateur,' she said. 'I own a boutique.'

'No shit!' Gwen blurted out. 'I mean, *wow*, I'd love to see it.'

Ann chuckled, and gave the steak one last whack.

The 'special friend' was due at eight, and Mom rushed through the door just a few minutes before. She was wearing a big red coat, a furry black hat, black riding boots and fire red lipstick. She looked — I didn't know what — *young*. There was a flurry of activity during which she dropped bags of gifts by the door, struggled out of her coat, hugged and kissed me, kissed Gwen, and greeted Ann and Betty. She tore around the kitchen making last minute preparations until the doorbell rang at eight, right on the button.

'Well?' she asked us, eyes glowing. 'How do I look?' She was wearing a tailored royal blue dress of raw silk.

I thought she looked pretty snazzy, but didn't want it to go to her head. So I said, 'You look okay, Mom,' and shrugged.

'You look like a million bucks!' Gwen said.

Ann laughed and snapped a dish towel at Mom. 'Go answer the door!'

We waited in suspense. There was a male voice, followed by silence. Kissing silence, I thought. Then Mom appeared in the doorway, smiling, and dragging a male hand. It was a mature, hairy hand with a white cuff and a grey sleeve. She tugged, and the rest of the body appeared.

It was Jerry O'Haran!

'Hi, Kate,' he said.

I didn't know what to say. I already knew I liked him, but I hadn't expected to see him attached to my mother's hand. In my mother's new apartment. The special guest.

'Kate,' Mom prodded, 'say hello to Jerry.'

I got up and shook his hand. 'Nice to see you,' I said, and sat back down.

'And it's very nice to see you again,' he said.

After dinner, as we cleaned up the kitchen, Mom asked me what I thought.

'It's not that I don't like the guy,' I said. 'But Mom, you're married.'

'Separated,' she corrected me, 'and getting divorced.'

'What about Dad?' I asked, though I knew how lame the question was. He had Lisa.

Mom said, 'Kate, I'm very happy and I was hoping you'd accept that. If you can't, then you'll just have to get used to it.'

'I *want* you to be happy, Mom.'

'Thank you, sweetheart. This isn't easy for Jerry, either. Or for me.'

'I know. I'm sorry.' And I was, and I wasn't. More than anything, my feelings were a jumble. I *did* want Mom to be happy — but with Dad.

Then Mom said, 'Why don't you think about inviting Patrick for New Year's?' and I understood that, despite separation, we were not all that distant. I was a girl at the beginning of love, she was a woman in the middle of it. To love a man — boy, male — outside the family would take invitations and diplomacy. She knew the value of an occasion like New Year's Eve. We were a little more like sisters now; consciously or not, she was becoming my conspirator. That obliged me to conspire with her, too: in return for her understanding, I owed her my own. I recalled the debt of reciprocity I sensed when Dad first brought me to Lisa. Now, Mom needed my approval too and was willing to reciprocate with hers. They were like lobbyists and I was Congress. They were giving me power over them, for the first time in my life. I liked it, in a way; but it didn't compete with the luxury of being a kid.

Dishes done, understandings struck, Mom and Jerry moved to the living room while Gwen, Ann and I sat at the dining room table stringing cranberries for the tree. Through the wide archway connecting the living and dining rooms, I could see them dancing. Jerry had taken off his tie and rolled up his sleeves. They had both kicked off their shoes.

Later, we all trimmed the tree. Jerry, a Catholic, crowned it with the Star of David I'd made from tin foil eight years ago. I liked him, I really did, but I could tell he wanted more, to be integrated into our lives. I didn't know if I could do it yet; it was still too soon.

He came back on Christmas Eve, then on Christmas Day. He gave me a gold chain necklace. I wore it out to dinner at a local restaurant, *Sun Foo Hunan*. It was Ann's idea to go Chinese. Ever since her own divorce, she said, she did something non-traditional on holidays. Plus, Chinese food was cheaper than going to a regular restaurant. It was one of the bylaws of divorce that budgets tightened when single mothers paid.

Gwen was wearing all eight Indian bangles I had given her, and every time she picked up her chopsticks, it sounded like the percussion section of a band. She had given me a makeup kit, and I had it all on my face. I felt bad about our argument in the bus station, now that I knew what it was all about.

Midway into the Hot and Spicy Chicken with Peppers, I became aware that Gwen was giving me a deadly look.

'What?' I said.

She noisily twirled cold noodles around a chopstick, and said nothing.

'Your mascara's running, dear,' Mom told me.

I touched my face and black came off on my fingers. Ann handed me a tissue and I wiped desperately.

'You look a lot better without makeup,' Jerry said. 'Some women just don't need it.'

Now, that was what I wanted to hear. I smirked at Gwen, and thanked Jerry. He was the first person to refer to me as a woman. I hoped Mom took note.

I called Patrick at school and invited him to join us for New Year's Eve. I also happily relayed Mom's message that he could stay with us for a few days. We were both excited about our rendezvous. I asked him if he was going to pass the exam this time. His answer was: 'Don't worry, I'll see you New Year's Eve.'

Plans for a quiet New Year's escalated into a party, and all of a sudden we were busy getting ready. We shopped and ate and cleaned and laughed. Mom, Ann, Gwen and I were like roommates. It was fun. Then Ann told Gwen and me that we could choose any dress from her boutique and borrow it for the night.

Ann's last name was Smith and her boutique, on Madison Avenue between 84th and 85th Streets, was *Smithereens*. She had two storefronts, with the adjoining wall knocked down. The walls were painted peach. Three glossy white pillars punctuated the open space. Track lighting sent dramatic shafts of light onto full-sized antique mirrors and vases of exotic paper flowers. Otherwise, it was all clothes.

I went straight for the wall with the fancy dresses. The first one that caught my eye was a flowing white gown, tapered at the waist and fanning out at the thighs. It had a long white scarf, the kind that killed Isadora Duncan, and when held up to the light, the dress sparkled.

'Hey, Ann!' I called. I held up the dress. 'I think there's a mistake on the ticket!'

'Thirteen hundred?' she said.

Shocked, I returned it to the rack and kept searching. There had to be something elegant but not so expensive that if I ruined it I'd be in debt for life. Mom and Ann sat on stools at the counter, talking and laughing. I could tell they were keeping an eye on us.

Gwen chose an orange jumpsuit that looked like a used aviator uniform. A band of thick elastic pinched her waist. Elephantine pants stopped inches above her ankles. A shapeless top zipped all the way above her head and fell over into an enormous collar. The sleeves were so long she had to roll them up. She thought she looked great. I thought she was crazy. Ann told her to choose any socks or stockings she wanted and keep them as a gift. Gwen took camouflage-print knee-highs.

I fell in love with a white dress of sheer lace with a Victorian collar, long lace cuffs and a built-in satin underslip that gave the dress a slinky feel.

'It looks like a wedding dress,' Mom said softly.

Gwen whispered, 'You look like some kind of prude!'

I ignored her, and selected real old-fashioned stockings — sheer white — and a garter belt. I knew just what I needed, and it wasn't a chastity belt. Mom was more right than she knew: tonight I would consummate my marriage.

Patrick was due at about six. Gwen and I spent the rest of the afternoon cleaning the apartment, while Mom and Ann dipped gourmet cookies into herb tea and talked about their ex-husbands. At one point — I missed the transition, being occupied with earthly matters such as chasing fast-moving tumbleweeds of dust — they switched to wine. Their whispered conversations would explode with laughter. I waited until a quarter past five to go into the kitchen and break up the pre-party party. They had everything laid out on the table: ceramic tea pot, tea cups smeared with chocolate, one empty and one almost-full wine bottle, two wine glasses also smeared with chocolate, and pads of paper on which they'd drawn cartoons and scribbled words. I caught a glimpse of Mom's pad before she flipped it over. Amidst the cartoons were two lists: *Pro* and *Con*. I glimpsed my name, but couldn't see which heading it fell under.

'Patrick's coming in less than an hour,' I reminded them.

'Lovely,' Ann said.

'He's a very nice boy,' Mom said. 'I've spoken with him on the phone, he has such a nice voice. I'll bet he's not bad looking, either.'

They laughed.

'He's very good-looking,' I said.

Their faces went serious and they stared at me.

'All I ask is that you clean up this mess and make yourselves presentable before six o'clock. Please.' I marched out of the kitchen and to the small bedroom, where Gwen stood in front of the door-mirror, intently teasing her limp hair. I heard the women's laughter from the kitchen.

I sat on my bed. 'It's almost five-thirty already.'

Gwen turned to me. Half her hair was electrified and the other half was lifeless. 'Relax. There's plenty of time. I mean, like, all you have to do is put on your clothes, right? Me, I have to do my hair, put on makeup and get dressed.' She held up three fingers.

'Gwen?'

'Ummm.'

'How many times have you, you know?'

She caught my eye in the mirror, and grinned. 'Say it.'

'You know what I mean.'

She teased out a section of hair before answering, 'Just that once.'

'When you got pregnant?' I was surprised; she had made herself out to be so worldly.

'Say it louder, why don't you!'

'What was it like? I mean, did it really hurt?'

She shrugged. 'Yeah, it hurt. But I figured you just had to get that part over with. They say it gets better. Why do you want to know?'

I picked at a hangnail on my little toe. 'Just curious,' I said. When I raised my eyes, I caught the last of her smile in the mirror.

'Happy New Year, Kate.'

# ELEVEN

The table was crammed with bowls of sticky black caviar, cornichons and olives, a half-moon of melty brie, a big basket of sliced French bread — or *baguette,* as Ann referred to it — and sparkly champagne glasses waiting to be filled. Ann dimmed the light so the glasses had a peachy glimmer, and the food practically glowed.

'Radiation alert!' Gwen said, lighting candle after candle — tall white flickering stalks — around the living room. 'These ladies really know how to live.'

Her hair was all teased and sprayed. And that orange bomber suit . . . she looked like Phyllis Diller in pajamas.

I was demure in my new borrowed dress, certainly more grown-up than Gwen as far as I was concerned. As she flitted around, lighting candles, I struck several poses to test my new self-consciousness, the new sensation of being an attractive woman.

'Think they'd mind if we had a drink before the party?' she whispered.

'I think they'd mind if we had a drink *during* the party.'

But Gwen was already dropping cubes of ice into two glasses, and filling them with vodka and orange juice.

'Cheers!'

'Happy New Year!'
And we drank.

Six o'clock came and went with no Patrick. At close to seven, Jerry arrived with two dozen red roses. Mom arranged them in a tall glass vase which she placed in the middle of the dining room table. All evening, as guests arrived, the roses were commented upon. 'They're from Jerry,' Mom would say. She would beam at him, wherever he was: standing next to her, or across the room talking to someone. They loved each other, that was clear. Their affection touched off all kinds of emotions in me: quick, deep feelings of loneliness, happiness, bewilderment, even jealousy.

One of the guests was a twenty-four-year-old woman named Eleanor. She was Russian royalty, a princess, or would have been had the Bolsheviks not interrupted the Czarist reign. She was American-born and had a heavy New York accent. '*Hoi,* she said, and a few giggles bubbled out of me. I knew it was mean to laugh, I just couldn't help it. Actually, I felt sorry for the woman. She had a distinct air of loneliness about her. She told me that she lived alone in a tenement apartment in the neighborhood, and had once worked in Ann's store. She was now employed as a secretary for an insurance company. In a sudden, conspiratorial moment, she told me that the one single man at the party — a fat lawyer with a ring of dark hair encircling a shiny bald spot like a monk's tonsure — had been invited for her. They were supposed to match up.

'Then why don't you go talk to him?' I asked her.

She shrugged her narrow shoulders. 'Nah,' she said. That must have been what she said to her mirror when she got ready to come over: *nah.* Her ash blond hair was pulled back with an elastic band, and under a plain brown skirt she was wearing old boots with holes at the sides where the width of her feet had worn through.

We were like a couple of Cinderellas before the ball. Waiting. Princess Eleanor and me, standing together by the caviar, in the foyer, in the kitchen doorway. I didn't know what she was waiting for. I, of course, was waiting for Patrick, and was beginning to have serious doubts that he would ever show.

Finally, I decided to call and find out. I excused myself, disappeared into Ann's bedroom, and dialed Grove.

The phone had rung into my ear twelve times, when the door creaked open and in walked Patrick! He looked pale and exhausted, as if he'd been running. He stood in front of me in his bluejeans, Frye boots and green sweater, and hooked his thumbs into his belt loops like an *aw shucks* cowboy returned from a distant prairie. He shrugged his shoulders and half-smiled.

'It took a while to get here,' he said. His smile stretched into a grin. 'You look beautiful.'

He bent down and kissed me very gently. As he pulled back, I leaned forward and kissed him again. Then I kissed him again and again and again.

'I'm so glad you came,' I said.

'Better late than never.'

I absently dropped the phone receiver on the pillow, and patted the spot next to me. He sat down and clasped his hands between his knees. He stared into the mirror on Ann's closet door: a cowboy and a virgin.

'You look like a bride,' he said, staring at my mirror-eyes.

He reached into his pocket and pulled out his fist. 'Do you still want me, us. . . I mean, do you remember what we said?'

My heart was pounding. Remember? I'd been doing nothing but waiting. And now, here it was New Year's Eve and Patrick was next to me, and I wanted nothing else.

'*Yes.*'

He flipped his fist, and his fingers uncurled. In the middle of his pinkish palm was a shining gold band. 'I hope it fits,' he said.

I hadn't expected a ring. It was beautiful, perfectly round, with a pinkish tint to the gold. I held out my left hand and he slid it down my fourth finger, but it was too big.

'I'll wear it on my middle finger,' I said. 'Anyway, that way no one will ask questions, but we'll know.'

He looked at me, uncertain whether I was just avoiding wearing the ring where it belonged — on my fourth finger — or compromising to circumstance. I knew then that he was afraid. I wasn't sure of what, exactly, but it was clear on his face. *Fear.* I had a terrible feeling that the main thrust of his fear was insecurity, and that he was at the door of his addiction again. Standing there, debating whether or not to open the door to the easy white gravityless world. Something inside of me, my heart or stomach, wrung with a desperate need to stop him. There was no place for me beyond that door. We had made vows to stand by each other, and the only place we could possibly do that was in my world, the one most people called reality which, if nothing else, was a world of unaltered states, of mutually-agreed upon points of perception. My mind was fixed on the physical consummation of our vows, on an image of solidly joining our bodies, a sharing of forces and of health. That was what I thought: that when we made love, something miraculous would happen to us and to him and to me. It had occurred to me that we would gain each other's strengths, but I had not imagined we would also share each other's weaknesses. The glow of despair in his eyes, as he slid the ring onto my finger, undercut my confidence. It was as if he didn't believe anything could make him whole, even me. I curled my fingers into my palm to keep the ring from falling off.

We leaned back onto the bed in a long, tight hug. His round face was all I could see: pale skin and dark blue eyes. He kissed my neck slowly, gently, and I drifted with the warm, peaceful sensations of feeling myself touched by him and touching him. Then I realized that the small, tinny voice of Silvera was speaking to me. Not to me, exactly, but into the phone. 'Hello?' he was saying in his gruff, unhappy voice. 'Hello? Hello! Hello!' Patrick froze and looked at the receiver lying on the pillow. Then he looked at me. There we were, on a bed, loving each other, with Silvera right there with us, but completely blind and helpless. We both started laughing hysterically. Silvera hung up with a fast, loud click.

It was a great moment, but it made me uneasy. I didn't want to take any chances of blowing our rendezvous, the real one, later.

'C'mon,' I said. 'Let's go in to the party.'

The living room buzzed with people. Patrick seemed nervous, so I held his hand and we walked over to Gwen. She was sitting on the couch with Princess Eleanor, who was pressed into the corner, listening. Gwen, of course, was doing all the talking. She was leaning forward, gesturing and laughing. She would break into quick smiles, giving her orange lipstick a real workout, and then throw her head back and start talking again. The princess looked scared. She glanced at Patrick and me, and nodded. I couldn't tell exactly what that nod meant: hello, or thanks for saving me.

'Hey!' Gwen said to Patrick. 'What the fuck kept you?'

'Gwen!' I protested.

'Lookit,' she said, 'everyone knows he's late. So big deal. Why not just get it right out in the open?' She looked at the princess for confirmation. 'Like, what I've been trying to tell you, El, is you have gotta learn to make it up as it comes along. Don't *worry* so much.'

Patrick leaned toward me and whispered, 'Can we have a drink?'

'Booze table's over there,' Gwen nearly shouted, pointing a stiff finger.

I said, 'Let's go say hi to Mom and Jerry. Remember Jerry, from Thanksgiving? He's Mom's boyfriend.'

'You're kidding me!'

'Nope, they — '

'Don't kid a kidder.'

We turned around. It was Ann. She was coming our way, dragging Jerry by the arm. He broke into his Mr Friendly smile, pumped Patrick's hand, slapped his shoulder. He said, 'Good to see you again, son!' His face was flushed. Ann's smile was larger than life. They were tipsy and I saw my chance.

'Think Mom would mind if we had a little champagne?' I asked.

Jerry surveyed our faces like a judge. 'Well,' he said, 'you're fifteen.'

'And a half.'

Jerry nodded. Motion carried. 'And you are how old?' he asked Patrick.

'Eighteen in May.'

Ann and Jerry both nodded. Jerry said, 'That would average the two of you out to about sixteen and three quarters each.' He looked at Ann.

'Between them they're close enough to legal age,' she said.

'All right, have a drink!' Jerry said.

Mom floated out from the kitchen in her black velvet caftan, like an earth mother from Planet Happiness. 'Hello, Patrick!' She kissed him lightly on the cheek, as if she already knew him, then wove her arm around Jerry's waist.

'You're only young and in love once, isn't that right?' Jerry asked Mom.

'The other times you're older.'

They laughed up a storm. I couldn't wait to get Patrick away from them.

'The children have requested, and received permission, to drink champagne tonight,' he informed her.

'Of course!' Mom must have been soused, too. 'Go! Don't waste your time with us oldsters.'

We poured ourselves champagne, drank one glass each, quickly, then refilled our glasses and sipped our way to the living room. We joined the princess at her station on the couch.

'Wouldn't you like some champagne?' I asked her.

'Oh, I'd love some!' Apparently, she had been too shy to

get some for herself. Patrick went to get her a glass.

'You have a very interesting friend,' she said to me. I looked at Patrick, thinking she meant him. 'No, your girlfriend,' she said.

'Oh, Gwen.'

The princess leaned over and snatched her purse from the floor. She zipped it open, dug around inside, and produced a plastic tag reading *the more people i meet, the more i like my cat,* from which dangled three keys. 'This one's for the front entrance, and these two are for my door.' She presented them to me.

'Why?'

She whispered: 'Your friend asked me if you could use my apartment for a few hours. Do you think you'll be finished by two o'clock? I'm a litle anemic, I get tired.'

I stared at her. Was she joking? Did Gwen really do this or was it some kind of sting operation?

'Go ahead,' the princess said. 'It's okay. At least I'll know someone had a good time in my apartment.' She smiled insecurely.

I took the keys.

Patrick returned with a glass of champagne, which he gave the princess. In return, she gave him a knowing smile.

I informed Mom that Patrick and I were going out for a walk. As we were putting on our coats, Gwen dashed over and pulled me into our bedroom.

'Jesus F. Christ,' she said, as she searched frantically through her suitcase. 'I know you haven't thought about precautions, Kate. It isn't so romantic when you get knocked up.' There was a fierce look in her eyes as she handed me a small foil packet.

'Strawberry flavored?'

'Use it.'

I slipped the condom into my coat pocket. 'Thanks.'

She winked.

Walking downtown on Second Avenue, toward 78th

Street where the princess lived, Patrick asked me what Gwen had wanted. I told him.

'I already thought of that,' he said. 'Don't worry.'

That shouldn't have surprised me, but it did. I knew in my logical, media-informed mind that birth control was something you were supposed to undertake with meticulous and unerring attention. In my other mind — the fifteen-year-old mind that was innocent of experience — it was something I could not bring myself to face. That should have told me I wasn't ready for sex. But it didn't. Because he had planned ahead, I told myself, I didn't have to. My thoughts had veered more to the abstract, not to blood and guts, conception and birth, contraception and abortion. I still saw sex as something beyond me, an obscure, unconnected, almost ethereal act suspended from the reality of life. It was still, to me, some kind of dreamy love bond, not a physical act with the capacity to root you to earth.

Slushy grey snow lined the avenue, splattering as cars whizzed past. It was after eleven and people were rushing to be somewhere, anywhere, when the clock struck twelve.

We turned the corner at 78th Street and headed toward First Avenue. Eleanor lived in two rooms of an old tenement building. We walked through her dark living room to the bedroom. Moonshine filtered through the windows, dousing the double bed in silvery shadows.

Patrick took off his army jacket and spread it over the bed, with the inside facing up. It took me a moment to understand that his plan was to stop the blood stain from permeating to the patchwork quilt. I felt a warm rush of trust. I had heard of girls whose innocence was either ridiculed or simply not believed by their men. I had heard of bitter accusations, and of girls who had sex just to prove their claim of virginity was true. With us, it was different. There was trust and love and desire, all the basic elements of emotion were there. Everything I felt then was strong, even if somewhat contradictory. Safety and fear. Excitement and numbness. Physical titillation and stinging pain. The thrill of gaining experience and despair at losing innocence.

Afterwards, we lay entwined, body and soul. Our breathing was grainy and slow, synchronized as an ocean gently lapping at sand. I thought he was asleep. Then he said, 'Does it hurt?' I nodded. He carefully drew himself out of me.

'Hold your legs together,' he said. He got up and went to the living room and I could see the shifting and flexing of muscle under his skin, the subtleties of his movement. Then his slender white body dissolved into silvery darkness. He reappeared with a roll of paper towels. He tore a bunch off and wadded them up.

'This will absorb it,' he said.

I pressed the wad of paper towels between my legs. Patrick lay next to me, leaning on his elbow, stroking my stomach. When the numbers on the digital clock on the bedside table flipped to read twelve, he leaned over and kissed me deeply. It was a long, warm, sexual kiss.

'Happy New Year.'

I combed my fingers through his messy hair. 'Happy New Year.'

We waited until the bleeding had mostly stopped before cleaning up and getting dressed. I found some Kotex in the princess's bathroom, and stuffed one into my underwear. Patrick promised he couldn't see a bulge through the dress. We were very careful. He washed the inside of his jacket and dried it with a hair blower we found. There was a stain, but it didn't show through to the other side. We put the paper towels and used condom in a shopping bag, which we deposited in a trash can on our way home.

It was not yet two o'clock. We decided we would say we'd walked all the way to Times Square and watched the old tradition of the lit-up ball descending slowly on a rod into the drunken cheering crowd.

Mom and Jerry had dozed off on the couch. Gwen was asleep in our room. Ann was cleaning up the kitchen. The only sign of a party was the two people who remained, sitting at the dining room table, drinking champagne and laughing. It was Princess Eleanor and the monk-haired lawyer. He was smiling, and his round cheeks were bright red. The princess was giggling. She was sitting with her legs crossed, tapping one worn boot excitedly in the air. When we walked into the room, she looked disappointed.

'Oh!' she said. 'It's late, isn't it?'

The man stood. 'Time to get going, yes.'

'Well,' the princess said meekly, 'it's been very — '

'May I walk you home?'

She seemed shocked. 'Thank you! Yes.'

The next day, we all piled into a cab and went to Rockefeller Plaza to skate. The pain between my legs didn't bother me; I felt elated, beautiful, unflappable. And Patrick, I thought, felt confident and excited, too.

The sky was overcast and everything looked grey, though now and then a cloud would move and sunlight would trickle through. It was warm out, and little by little scarves unwound and zippers came apart. By the time we had rented skates and put them on, it was too hot, and we all abandoned our jackets to the coatcheck. Patrick carefully folded his jacket so the stain wouldn't show. This thrilled me; it was our special secret. He held my hand as we maneuvered the blades of our skates over the rubberized surface to the rink.

Once onto the ice, Patrick kissed me on the forehead and then sped away, his bright green sweater blending into the colorful tapestry of the skaters. I moved slowly along the railing, catching occasional glimpses of Patrick or Gwen ripping along. She'd traded in her white ladies' skates for a pair of boys' black racers. Except for the skates, she was dressed all in white: white jeans, white sweater, white scarf. Her blond hair sailed behind her. Her speed and confidence made me want to tell her about last night. I tried to catch up with her, but she made a sudden turn and I crashed into a couple who had been skating arm-in-arm. They sneered, scrambled up and glided away. I was like a beached whale sitting on the ice, frantic amidst a blur of skaters. Then Patrick's green flashed out of the human potluck. He lifted me up in one swift movement and steadied me with an arm around my waist.

'You really stink at this,' he said.

'It's been years,' I lied. I'd been skating every winter of my life but had never gotten the hang of it.

Mom and Ann didn't even bother trying. They sat on the sidelines drinking cocoa and talking. They were both wearing skates as if they were high heels, sitting casually crosslegged, swinging their feet. Jerry was loitering by the railing, catching his breath. When Patrick and I skated past them, Mom started calling out to us, and Ann and Jerry joined in. 'Go, Speed Racer!' 'Ginger and Fred!' 'Hey, do it, kids!' Everybody looked. It was terrible. When we were halfway around the rink, Jerry and Gwen sailed past us, skating backwards and sticking out their tongues. It was a wonderful day. Patrick told me seven times that he loved me. The thrill of being lovers was all I needed; I could go on and on without sleep or food. I was dying to tell Mom we were married, but knew, even in my love-delirium, that there was no way she would take us seriously, especially since a snowman had done the honors. No, we would go on being lovers in secret. We would share each other's bodies in perfect, private friendship, on the leaf-matted floor of a shadowy forest, under a bridge, on a borrowed bed.

After skating, we went to the movies and saw *Lady Sings the Blues*. It was the story of Billy Holliday, and Mom had been dying to see it. The beautiful woman makes the world fall in love with her, and then destroys herself with heroin. I had told Mom all about Patrick when I ran away from school. Was this her way of telling me something, of expressing disapproval or concern? She made no indication that she even remembered. But I did. And so did Patrick.

Later, he asked me if there was supposed to be a hidden message.

'Like what?'

We were sitting on the living room couch, our first moment alone all day. He was leaning back into the cushions, and his leg was bent between us, creating a barrier.

'Why wouldn't anyone look at me after the movie?' he asked.

'No one was looking at anyone,' I said. 'Patrick, I haven't advertised your problem.'

'Problem? Is that what it is?'

'Well — '

'I've been straight.' He bared his palms as if to say, *look, nothing hidden.*

'But Patrick,' I leaned toward him, 'there's nothing to worry about. I don't care what anybody thinks.'

'But they know. They know about me.'

'I guess I mentioned it to Mom when I ran away. I was scared.'

Sighing, he said, 'Kate — ' then stopped himself, and shook his head in defeat. But who had defeated him? Had it really been me? The thought that he could feel I would contribute to his sense of defeat terrified me.

'But I love you,' I said. 'I would never do anything behind your back. It doesn't matter if Mom knows, because you're straight now. I mean, everyone has something to be ashamed of.'

'Do you?'

'I don't know. Probably. I'm not perfect.'

'But you are. You know just what to say. Even now.'

'I try — '

'That's right. You try too hard. Kate, you seem to think that just because we made love last night, everything's okay now. It isn't, it *isn't*. How can it be?' He stared at me, his eyes fury-blue, a storm.

'How can it *not* be?'

'Kate,' he whispered, 'I ran away from school to get here to see you. I failed the test. Now I can't go back.'

My gaze fixed on his bouncing knee. I couldn't think of

anything to say; my brain was numb, my stomach churned, I was crashing.

'You're too idealistic,' he whispered in a deep, insistent voice. 'It doesn't mean I don't love you, though.'

'What *does* it mean?'

He shook his head, shrugged. Lone cowboy, about to make his getaway. 'I just won't see you for a while,' he said. 'There's no way around it.'

'Then how could you come here last night? How could you?'

He grabbed my arm and pulled me forward. Staring straight into my eyes, pinning my attention down, he said, 'I had to come here last night. I had to see you. I promised.'

I had gotten too high, too happy, too fast, and now I was knocked lower than ever. I couldn't cry, could hardly feel anything other than sick to my stomach. 'But Patrick — ' I started, unable to find words to complete the sentence, let alone the thought. *But Patrick. How could you leave me? How could you claim me with such devotion and then tell me you're going away?*

Finally I said, 'Are you going to try to get back into school?'

'I don't know. I haven't decided yet.'

'Where will you go?'

'I'll stay with a friend for a while.'

'Who?'

One side of his mouth curled up. 'Listen Kate, I'm sorry this is happening. I hope you'll be able to forgive me. I really want you to believe that I love you very much.'

'I guess I believe it.'

'You don't need to guess.'

I rolled the ring around my finger, feeling the cool, smooth surface, deciding. Finally, I took it off and put it on the cushion between us. 'This really has been a farce, hasn't it?'

Worry lines etched his forehead. 'No,' he said. 'Please, keep that.'

I left it on the couch for a few moments before picking it up and holding it in my hand. When it was warm from the heat of my palm, I held it out to him. 'Would you wear it?' I asked.

He hesitated, but then took the ring. It fit perfectly on his pinky.

He promised: 'I'll never take it off.'

# TWELVE

Patrick had run away from school and robbed a newsstand to get the money to come see me New Year's Eve. That information circulated quickly enough through school. But there was more, things only I knew, from two brief phone conversations with him. He admitted to 'borrowing' Tamara the cook's wedding ring from her campus apartment. She was divorced and kept the ring in a small enamel box in her living room. Patrick visited her during the first few days of winter break. When she left the room to answer the phone, he happened to open the box and see it. The ring. Perfectly round, pink-gold, a band of eternity that would hug his pinky forever. He never returned it, and I never told; it was one of our special secrets.

Another secret was that he was staying with Eddie's family in Brooklyn. Actually, Patrick didn't come right out and tell me this; he must have known it would upset me to hear he was in touch with Eddie, let alone living with him. He casually mentioned walking across the Brooklyn Bridge, and I guessed the rest. But he swore he was straight, and that Eddie was out of trouble. They were both working in a bakery and had learned to make bread. He was terrified of anyone finding out where he was and turning him in to the police for robbing the newsstand. And taking the ring. And running away from school. Not to mention having slept with me. I was only fifteen. Once the authorities discovered his history with drugs, that would have been the end: of his freedom, his youth, us.

I promised never to tell, and I didn't. I protected Patrick with all my heart. He had hurt me, and I was angry that he hadn't told me the truth before we went to the princess's apartment. But I loved him. I was *in love* with him; there was no way I could betray him.

Then one day, Eddie was arrested for dealing drugs. He was fined and put on probation. Patrick claimed it was pot, but the rumor around school was that it was also smack — heroin, the mean stuff. Patrick assured me that he was not involved in any way, selling or using. He even offered to let me speak with Mrs Cohen to confirm the story. I didn't want to; I was trying to trust him. But trusting an addict with the truth is like trusting a jewel thief to guard the palace door. He'll guard it, all right; no one will get past but him.

January was cold and bleak and lonely. The landscape was slender, naked trees perched on frozen dirt, under a grey sky streaked with darkness by mid-afternoon. It barely snowed. The Reverend White melted into a nondescript lump on the science field. I would stand there and remember in exact detail the exchange of our vows. I could remember everything: Patrick's face through the small opening of his hood, the way his hands (in black gloves) were clenched at his sides, the bite of the wind, the clouds of frozen breath with each word. I never cried, and sometimes I didn't feel anything. I just stood there. The snowman melted into a wet spot on the ground, then into nothing.

I was there one late afternoon, just before dinner, when I heard the sound of footsteps crunching on the frozen earth behind me. They were steady, controlled steps that got louder as they descended the hill, and stopped just behind me.

'This would be the perfect spot,' a voice said.

I turned around and there was Peter Prentice, straight as a pole with his arms flush at his sides. He looked tiny under his huge blue pea coat. A grey driving cap sat awkwardly on his head of straight brown hair. His gloveless hands were bright red. When he smiled, the small, refined features of his face remained perfectly still.

'What?' I asked.

'This would be the perfect spot for the dome.'

Oh, the dome. That ridiculous project of his.

I braced myself against a sharp gust of wind. He closed his eyes and exhaled slowly. Very softly, he said, 'If you just relax, you won't be cold.'

'It's freezing out here, Peter.'

He opened his eyes. They were dark blue, like Patrick's, but with lush brown lashes. He said, 'To a degree.'

I couldn't resist smiling at that, but I quickly suppressed it. I didn't want him to think I was being friendly; he was a loony, after all.

'It must be about time for dinner,' I said.

'It's four minutes before six o'clock,' he told me without looking at his watch (if he even had one). 'Dinner is at — '

'Yeah, I know, six o'clock.'

He looked toward the barren science field, calmly, as if such quiet and emptiness were so familiar they didn't intimidate him. I felt a stab of pain — *his* pain. I assumed he was very lonely. Then I realized that, despite my assumptions, I didn't have the slightest idea of who he really was.

'There are approximately one-and-a-half minutes left before returning to central campus is utterly necessary,' he said. 'I would rather spend it here, thinking about the dome.'

'Well, I'll see you around, then.'

He nodded. His face was expressionless, strangely peaceful. I didn't know why, but I was tempted to stay with him for that extra ninety seconds.

'Please don't feel concerned about leaving me here alone,' he said. 'I feel fine.'

I wanted to ask: *but how?* Or say: *bullshit, liar, I have friends and a boyfriend* (absent if not former; I didn't know just to what degree Patrick was gone) *and I'm dying of loneliness! How can you feel fine, when you don't have a single friend?*

What I said was, 'What is a geodesic dome, anyway?'

I saw a flash of gratitude in his eyes. No one had ever asked him.

'According to the Random House dictionary, it is a light, dome-like structure developed to combine the structurally desirable properties of the tetrahedron and the sphere.'

'Uh huh. Could I ask you another question, more personal?'

'There's time for one more.'

'Why do you want to build one? I mean, what for?'

This time I saw a flicker of pleasure. He had probably been aching to tell someone. He said: 'It's my dream.'

A few days later I saw Peter walking into the field after his physics class. He was only in ninth grade, but took twelfth grade physics; he was a real brain when it came to science. Patrick had also been in physics, which was why I knew what the class next door to my biology class was. It was the last period before lunch, and Patrick or I — whoever got out first — would wait so we could walk up to lunch together. Now, alone, I stopped before going up the hill for lunch and watched Peter walking into the distance so steadily that he appeared to be gliding. When he reached the middle of the field, he stopped. He stood very still, as if rooting himself into the ground. Then, after a minute of absolute quiet, he lifted his face and screamed.

I recognized it immediately. It was the same scream I had heard the night Patrick was expelled for heroin. Standing alone by the road in the dark, suddenly there was that scream. It was the scream that had jolted me back to my senses. I had run up the hill to the dorm, and Gwen had told me the truth about Patrick. I had claimed the disembodied scream as my own. I felt that scream in the bottom of my soul. It was Peter's scream.

His high, clear voice echoed. When it faded, he turned around and glided in my direction.

'Hello,' he said in a mild voice, completely devoid of the passion of his scream.

'Are you all right?'

A faint pink colored his ivory skin. 'I have released myself,' he said.

Then and there, I decided to help him build his crazy dome.

# PART THREE

# THIRTEEN

At best, the dome was oddly meaningful; at least, it was something to focus on besides Patrick or myself. Patrick. I worried about him, and especially I missed him. His sea blue eyes. His carrot top. His damp palm pressing against my back. His gravelly voice, whispering, *Kate, Kate*. A fountain of laughter, loud and free. Sudden anger. He was always there, in the back of my mind. But as the days and weeks passed, I grew less tormented by his absence. The single thing that caused me stinging, unending pain was the memory of New Year's Eve. That memory, more than anything else, aggravated my loneliness. It was like a light shining on a well of darkness on the edge of which I stood, alone, staring down. The image I conjured up to help me sleep was of a dome covering the mouth of the well, preventing me from falling in.

The setting sun drew a veil of orange and purple over the science field. The air was biting cold, but there was a feeling of great calm.

'The first thing you have to do,' I told Peter, 'is figure out exactly how much it's going to cost.'

'It will cost what it will cost,' he said.

'Yeah, okay, but you need an idea of what it's going to amount to. I mean, who's going to give you the money to build it if they think it might cost a million dollars in the end?'

'It probably won't cost that much to build.'

'Well? How much *will* it cost?'

'Less than a thousand dollars, certainly.'

'How much less?'

He thought. 'I would calculate that it could be as much as seven hundred dollars less.'

'You're telling me the dome would cost about three hundred bucks to build?'

'Possibly. Approximately. Yes.'

Peter was far from practical enough to deal with the nitty gritty details. No wonder he never got his dome built! I *was* practical, so I took over the planning. I became Vice President of Dome Inc., in charge of fundraising and development. Peter was President, in charge of vision and spirit.

I called local lumber yards and plastics manufacturers from the pay phone in the school building. Based on Peter's assessment of what he would need to build the dome, I came up with an estimated cost of two-hundred thirty-seven dollars. Since we would build it ourselves, there was no cost for labor.

Ted suggested we speak with Silvera about requisitioning funds from the activities budget. When I told Peter, it struck him like a revelation. I was amazed that he had been so sure his dome would be built without ever considering how.

It was faith, he told me. He said, 'There was never any doubt in my mind that the dome would be constructed. The karma of the project had been waiting for you to become ready to help.'

'Me? You mean, you knew all along I'd get involved?'

'The dome's karma knew.'

I hoped the dome's karma had also gotten through to the man, because I didn't expect him to dig right into the school's pocket on my account or Peter's. He had known about Peter's idea all along, as had everyone else, but had never offered to help.

Silvera held court every afternoon after activities. I was taking dance in the gym and dashed up to the dorms afterwards to change. I wanted to be the first to Silvera's room; otherwise, someone else might grab his attention until dinner. I was peeling off my leotards, when Gwen and Rawlene came in wearing wire baskets over their faces. They were taking fencing. I thought they looked like bees.

I bent over and gave my hair a few whacks with the brush from underneath, then flipped back to standing. 'How do I look?'

'Why are you getting dressed so soon?' Gwen asked.
'What time is it?'

'Just past five,' Rawlene said.

'Got a date with Peter?' Gwen asked.

'Peter?' Rawlene echoed. 'That skinny weirdo kid? I'll box his ears if he thinks he's gonna get in Kate's pants.' She crossed the room and stood in front of my dresser, where Patrick's framed picture sat. Leaning her elbows on the dressertop, she gazed at the photo.

Gwen flashed a wink at me. 'Kate wants to help him build that dome thing,' she said. 'But don't spread it around. We don't want anyone to get the wrong idea.'

'We?'

'I am not ashamed to say,' Gwen said, 'that I have been considering joining the team.'

No way. The dome was mine, it was not for sharing. I pulled on a pair of black pantyhose and shoved my feet into my shoes.

'I have to go.'

'Kate, wait a minute.'

I turned in the door and looked at her. She was smiling: innocent, kniving Gwen. What was she up to now?

'I mean it,' she said. 'I want to help.' She stared at me through her face net. I could just barely see the expression that had so often persuaded me. That face guard made her look so ridiculous, I laughed.

'Please?'

She'd probably bring the BHBs to sing and dance and distract us. Plus, I was sure she didn't understand Peter Prentice. No one did, maybe not even me. But I, at least, wanted to protect him from the loony-mongers. I no longer thought he was so strange.

'Maybe,' I said.

'You'll think about it? Really?'

'Sure,' I lied. 'I'm late, gotta go.' I clipped my hair back with a barrette, then spirited out of the room.

Peter met me in the lobby of Lower Girls. We had agreed to wear good clothes, thinking Silvera might take us more seriously dressed up. Peter's pants were huge, with a canvas belt pinching them around his waist. His white shirt was buttoned all the way to his Adam's apple. He had wetted and combed his hair so it lay perfectly flat.

'You look very pretty,' he said, and offered me an arm. 'Shall we?'

We walked down the hall like a prom couple, nervous and overdressed, trying to contain our anxious breathing in the slow rhythm of our steps.

Silvera's door was cracked an inch and we pushed it all the way open. There he was, lying on his back on the floor with his arms spread wide, as if he were flying. His eyes were closed.

'Hello?' I said.

His nostrils flared. He grunted.

'It's Kate Steiner and Peter Prentice.'

The man's eyes snapped open, and he twisted around to look at us. I think he was more interested in the fact that we had come together than what we had come about. He sat up clumsily. He nodded his head rapidly, nostrils flared, dark eyes burning with life.

'Yes,' he said, 'very interesting.'

Peter spoke nervously in a high, nasal voice. 'We are here — '

I cut him off: 'Can we come in?'

Silvera gave one quick nod of his head.

I sat crosslegged on a bean bag and Peter stood like a pole at my side.

Peter said, 'We are here — '

'The dome, right?' Silvera broke in. 'Why are *you* here?' he asked me.

'I'm going to help Peter build it,' I said. 'We need to buy some supplies. We wanted to ask if we could get some money from the activities fund.'

He looked at Peter, then back at me. 'Where do you want to put it?'

'The science field. We figured that would be the perfect place, plus teachers could use it in their courses.' The thought had just occurred to me, but it seemed like a good selling point, so I threw it in.

'How big?' Silvera asked.

Peter answered, 'Life size.'

Silvera smiled. 'How much will it cost?' he asked Peter, though he must have known better than anyone that Peter would not have come up with a figure. That was when I realized that Silvera had never been against the project, Peter had simply never asked.

'Considerably less than it might seem,' Peter said.

I said: 'Two-hundred thirty-seven dollars, on the nose.'

Silvera nodded thoughtfully. Then he said to me, 'Too bad about Patrick,' and watched my face for a reaction.

I could feel my eyes watering, the dam breaking. I couldn't help it. I wanted to run, but couldn't move. Yet I also felt curiously safe. Without Peter there, I never would have cried in front of the fat man. Then it struck me that maybe he was testing Peter, to see if he could handle being partners with such an emotionally volatile girl.

Peter shifted toward me like a reed leaning in the wind. He said softly to Silvera, 'We will work every afternoon during activities and the dome will be completed by spring.'

'Kate,' Silvera said, 'is that schedule okay with you? No problem with it?'

'I'll be here, won't I?'

'Give me a finishing date.'

'The twelfth of April,' Peter said with surprising specificity.

'Why the twelfth?' Silvera asked.

'May I answer with a rhetorical question?'

Silvera waved a hand in the air, and said, 'Get me a breakdown of cost and suppliers, and I'll have checks for you tomorrow after classes.'

Peter's porcelain face cracked a smile. 'Thanks.'

The next afternoon, when Peter and I were to meet to pick up the checks, I found Junior, a Little Kid, alone in the lobby of Lower Girls. I had always liked Junior. He was eight years old and small for his age, with twiggy limbs, and a large round head covered with short, frizzy black hair. He had the curliest eyelashes, and brown skin as soft as feathers. He was just sitting there, lost in a tattered green armchair.

'Hi, Junior!'

He didn't even smile.

'Have you seen Peter Prentice?'

He shrugged his tiny shoulders.

'Mind if I wait with you?'

'Naw.'

I sat on the arm of the chair, and he stared up at me. He was like a magician whose big, sad eyes pulled me down into the chair. I tried to squeeze in next to him. He wiggled into my lap, wrapped his little arms around my neck, and dropped his head on my shoulder.

'What's wrong, Junior?'

'My mama was supposed to call me up.'

'She didn't call?'

He shook his head.

'Why don't you call her?'

'I ain't got no money.'
'Call collect. That means she pays.'
His head sprang up. 'You know how?'
'I'll show you.'

He hung onto me like a bur all the way to the pay phone in the hallway. When I tried to set him down, he clung. 'Just stand here for a minute,' I said. 'What's her number?'

He shook his head.

'What's her name?'

'Flower Booker.'

'Where does she live?'

'She lives with my daddy's friend in the Bronx.'

'What's his name?'

'Rico Nez.'

I found his number easily through Information. I placed a call collect from Junior, and a nasty man refused to accept charges.

'Looks like no one's home,' I told him.

I took his hand and led him back to the chair.

'I have to go find Peter,' I said. 'Where's Alfonse or Bobby?' They were his best friends.

'They're at basketball.'

'Don't you have an activity to go to?'

He shook his head. 'I don't want to bake no cakes.'

'You signed up for Home Ec?'

'Nobody told me we be bakin' cakes. I thought we be goin' home.'

*Ec.* How was Junior supposed to know it meant economics? The domestic arts. What a corny thing to teach Grovers! They should have taught Street Ec, or Running Away Ec, or Addiction Ec — something that would have been useful to our lives. Junior was right: baking cakes wouldn't help.

I didn't know how long Peter was standing in the doorway before I noticed him. He had been watching us.

'Good,' he said. 'That will be very good.'

'What?'

'Junior will be an asset to the dome.'

Junior sprang up. 'Me? Me?' He balanced on the edge of the chair, watching my face, waiting for a reaction.

Peter was right: Junior's impish spirit would be just right for our quirky dome. Not to mention the fact that we could lord it over him, since he was so much younger than us. He could run errands, bring us nails and sodas.

'Okay,' I said. 'Let's go ask.'

Junior waited in the lobby while we went in to see Silvera. He was lying on the floor again. He must have felt our presence, because he immediately said, 'The envelope's on the table. Take it.'

'Excuse me,' I said. 'But can we ask you a question?'

'Both of you together, or are you schizophrenic now?'

I rolled my eyes at Peter. He took over. 'Mr Silvera, sir, we would like to make a special request on behalf of Junior Booker.'

Silvera grunted.

'If Junior could assist us in building the dome, a double purpose would be accomplished. One, we would have a helper. And two, Junior would get early experience in working on a construction crew.'

'And three,' I threw in, 'he might not miss his mother so much.'

Silvera didn't like item three. Grove was supposed to be enough for anyone, you weren't supposed to need your parents at Grove.

'Junior Booker's mother is a call girl,' Silvera said, his eyes still peacefully closed.

Peter and I looked at each other. My first thought was that it wasn't true. Junior himself had mentioned his father, and if his mother was a prostitute, then she probably wouldn't even know who the father was. Anyway, so what? All Junior had done was get born — and have the misfortune of landing at Grove.

Finally, the man grunted, 'Go ahead.'

When we told Junior, he jumped off the chair and went running to his room. He came back wearing a green jacket, a red baseball cap and a huge smile. He was thrilled. And I was curious (so was Peter, I think) about his parents. I asked him what his father looked like. He said, 'Well, my daddy has dark light skin, and kind of these nice blue eyes, and he has hair all curly just like mine but it be blond, and my mama she says he plays the blues, and he be a banker in a bank. But me, I always lived with Rico Nez. She says he's my daddy's friend. He be ugly.'

That was Junior's dream, I guess. For him, the dome would provide more real family than he had ever had. And what was my dream? To forget. To capture an old dream, and to forget it.

Waiting in the science field for deliveries, I looked over and saw Gwen standing on the hill looking down at us: me and Peter and Junior. She didn't wave or nod or shout; she just stood there like a statue, wearing her fencing outfit and carrying a sword. Gwen the warrioress. After a few minutes, she walked away.

I knew that when she found out Junior was helping us, after refusing *her* help, she'd be mad. And she was. And hurt, too. Why did I do it? After all, we'd had fun over winter vacation, reforged our friendship. I wasn't sure why I was closing her out. But since knowing me, Peter watched Gwen, too. He had a theory. According to him, I had an impulse toward loneliness, which was why I had rejected Gwen's offer to work on the dome. His theory was that I wanted her to work with us, but had rejected her in an effort to reinforce my feelings of loss over Patrick; that if I let her all the way into my heart, I wouldn't feel so awful so much of the time; and if I didn't feel awful, I would be abandoning Patrick. In other words, said Peter, I was rejecting Gwen so I could feel closer to Patrick.

All I knew was that I was drawn to the hard labor of building something. And that I liked Peter: he was my new friend. I was his only friend. There were no demands, just peaceful afternoons, and the rising structure of the dome.

The dome would be built of balsa wood and plastic triangles. The materials themselves were lightweight, but the geometric dynamic of the structure — frame and plastic — was supposed to make it strong as a whole. It was a *holistic* endeavor: structurally, in that the integrity of the whole depended upon the integrity of each part; and spiritually, in that the dome's success depended on our individual commitments to doing it and doing it right. We did everything slowly and carefully. If the dome wasn't precise in every way, it would collapse like a house of cards.

First, we plotted the base. Peter had worked out all the measurements long ago and stored them in his head. He used a measuring tape to determine exactly where each joint in the base structure should be, and I would place a stone in that spot. It took a whole afternoon to lay the stones, but when we were finished, we had marked out a perfect circle on the frozen ground. It was like our own mini Stonehenge. The mystery was fun. Kids would stand on the hill, watching. All they knew was that we were building a dome; they didn't know how or why. A few of them thought I had gone crazy. I know. Gwen told me.

It took two weeks to establish a perfectly symmetrical foundation and customize the pieces of wood. Day to day, I thought more about the perfection of the dome and less about Patrick: where he was, if he was all right, when (if) he was coming back. Sawing a board at a precise angle demanded total concentration. Everything had to be right. Peter and I cut the wood and Junior made neat, organized piles in an empty classroom. Then, during the second week, a snow storm came. By then we had built the base — a web-like circle of triangles — and it rose above the smooth expanse of snow like a jagged ring on a cloud.

Early in February, there were four more storms. Each time, Junior shoveled all around the work area. It was freezing out, and the snow he accumulated off to the side didn't melt, it just kept building into an ever-larger mound. While Peter and I were busy tapping nails into the joints of wood, Junior started a snowman. He was supposed to be sorting nails, but he was only eight; I guess he just couldn't resist. It was a little snowman — a snowboy about eight years old, I'd say, and just Junior's height. He gave it nuts for eyes, a nail for a nose and two nails in a V for a mouth. The snowboy's arms were twigs, and to keep his head warm, Junior made a sailor's hat from a piece of newspaper.

'Meet my brother,' Junior said when he was finished. 'His name's Senior.'

But for me, he was the Reverend White. He had to be. He watched us like a sentry guarding the rebuilding of a burned-down house, overseeing an important resurrection.

It was around that time that I dreamed of Patrick's arm. He was sleeping next to me in a bed — I don't know where — and he was naked, lying on his side, facing me. His arm was stretched over the pillows, as if reaching for me, pale and graceful and speckled with tiny red marks. It was his heroin arm — the other woman — and it appeared beautiful to me. It was like a constellation of stars behind which lay a myth: the meaning was love, and though it was love for something other than me, it was deeply moving. Here was my husband, reaching toward me with great and passionate love, telling me with his arm that intrinsic to his love for me was a threat.

I woke up knowing that it was his love for *her* — for heroin — that had stolen him from me. The knowledge hit like a knife in my heart. The dream twisted the knife, and all my pain came pouring out like a gush of blood. The one I had vowed to love forever was gone. Vanished into addiction.

I started bumming cigarettes from people that day. It was as if the smoke could cauterize my pain, clog me, numb me from my loneliness for him. Patrick had made a choice. When he stole from the newsstand, even though it was to come and see me, he knew what the consequences would be. He knew he would have to leave. I understood that he felt pain, and that his addiction was a restless drive that had existed in him before he knew me. But I still couldn't shake the feeling that I had been cheated.

Working on the dome became an obsession: seeing it finished was my only hope. It was a chance to create something special in the place of emptiness. *A dream.* It was almost as if, when the dome was finished, I would live in it, and it would protect me from further loss.

By now, a thick layer of snow covered the ground, and the dome's skeleton rose in a web of footsteps. A layer of ice preserved Senior the snowboy (my Reverend White), and he guarded the dome and us unfailingly in his frozen paper hat.

Then, one day, Senior the snowboy started to melt. A muddy moat surrounded the dome where we had worn down the snow. It was early, and I was working alone. I heard the slush of footsteps coming down the hill and assumed it was Peter or Junior.

'Could you do me a favor, Kate?'

I turned around. Gwen's blue hat was tugged down to her eyebrows. She smiled, but it wasn't genuine. She was upset.

'What's wrong?' I asked.

She pulled an envelope out of her coat pocket and clumsily withdrew a folded letter.

'Could you just read this, please?' she said.

I unfolded it, and read.

> Dear Kate,
> I would like to point out to you that you're being xxxxxxxxx unfair. Deep down you are holding a grudge against me for something I didn't do. If I did you wrong once well everyone deserves forgiveness and I thought you had forgiven me, especially after Xmas (which was a lot of fun). It isn't my fault if P. is gone, that is, he is gone due to his own mistakes not mine. I would like to remind you that I am true to you. Plus I need you right now. What I'm trying to say is please forgive me, really forgive me (even if I'm innocent) because I am willing to be your ultra best friend 4 ever. 4 real. Gwen

P.S. My father is coming up for Parents' Day. I think I'll die.

P.P.S. The dome looks good.

Gwen thrust her hands into her jacket pockets and shivered against the cold. She watched me, and waited.

Peter was right: I had fallen in love with my loneliness. My dream of Patrick had filled me with pain and desire and hopelessness, and I had resisted any bridge back to friendship.

She broke into a big smile. Her whole face glowed at me, and she winked. She was pulling a *Gwen,* making herself more irresistible than my loneliness. I smiled back at her, I couldn't help it. And without making any conscious decision, I handed her my hammer.

# FOURTEEN

Parents' Day was Silvera's big chance to make an impression. Our parents' money, after all, funded his opportunity for an obscure brand of leadership. But real leaders do not turn to confused adolescents, they speak directly to adults. Not Silvera. His line changed on Parents' Day; he didn't talk about 'dealing with your shit,' but about grades, and grounds, and graduates. He got himself a haircut and a shave, and wore a suit and tie. What a big joke. If our traditional values were so strong, we wouldn't have been at Grove. We were all pretending. We knew our parents didn't want us; *why* was irrelevant. And our parents didn't really care how spic-and-span the place was or how well-dressed we were. Parents' Day was marked on the school calendar; it was a requirement on both sides, that was all. I hated it, before it even happened. To me, it was just a reminder of how awry our lives had gone.

Dad was coming at one, and Mom at three-thirty. I put on a green plaid skirt, black turtleneck, blue kneesocks, and old penny loafers. I didn't even brush my hair again after breakfast. I just lay on my bed reading Camus' *The Stranger*, while Gwen buzzed around the room, doing herself up. She curled her hair and searched through her wardrobe. Finally, she settled on a red knit dress that hugged her slender hips and clung to her sharp, tiny breasts. I didn't understand it. Why would she want to look pretty for her father when she claimed not to want to see him?

Rawlene came in and the two of them stood in the bathroom making up their faces. Then Amy burst into the room, wearing a blue dress crawling with wild red flowers. 'Get ready!' she said, and made way for a fat little girl with tightly cornrolled hair. She had a round chocolate face and wore a lacy yellow dress. A big yellow bow sat on top of her head.

'Meet my iddy biddy sister Marigold.'

Rawlene dashed over to the little girl and bent down to eye-level. 'I'm Rawlene, your sister's very best friend outside'a Nicky and you, sweetpea. I've been waitin' to meet you. I hear you've got one helluva singin' voice.'

In a high, clear voice, Marigold said, 'Amy, she says I be a Butterfly'f I want.'

'Baby, you're a Butterfly. Lookin' at you, I just know it.'

A vision of Marigold's bow flapping and carrying her into the air made me smile. Marigold looked at me and smiled back.

'This is Kate,' Rawlene said. 'She's a friend of Gwen, who's a Butterfly, too.'

Gwen stood in the bathroom door, her blond hair hanging in limp curls, her poppy-red lips smiling. 'Hi!' she said.

'You a honky,' Marigold said, and that stopped us all cold. She couldn't have been more than four, a little seedling already sprouting racism. Marigold walked over to Gwen and touched her hand. 'She so soft.'

Gwen leaned over and tugged at either side of Marigold's bow. 'And you're cute,' she said.

We all laughed.

I dog-eared my book and sat on the edge of my bed. A huge black man in a blue suit stood in our doorway. Marigold flew into his arms, crying, 'Daddy!' He nodded somberly as Amy introduced us. Then he turned and walked away, toting Marigold in his arms.

Amy rolled her eyes, whispered, 'Sorry, girls,' and left.

Rawlene shrugged and went after them, mumbling, 'Gotta go.'

'The man's a fucking prig!' Gwen said. 'Those are my friends. He can't do this to me.' And she dashed after them.

The room seemed so quiet all of a sudden. The window was open a crack and I could hear whole families passing by, chattering, laughing, getting the grand tour. I felt a strong pang of loneliness — for *my* family, which today I would receive in splinter factions — and wandered out into the lobby to see who was there.

A few kids sat around, waiting, and a lot of traffic moved between the hallways and front door. A man sat on the couch in his coat and hat, looking nervously around, tapping his thumbs together. He had a pudgy, shaven face and dim blue eyes. He looked familiar. I stared at him for a minute before realizing that it was Mr Perle, Gwen's father. Where was she? I didn't know what to do, so I just stood there, pretending to be nonchalant, trying my best to check him out. I noticed that his wedding ring was missing. He looked sad.

I couldn't help it: I walked right up to him, smiled, and said, 'Hi, I'm Kate, I room with Gwen.'

He stood up and shook my hand. His felt damp and clammy. Then we sat next to each other on the couch.

'You look familiar,' he said. His voice was smooth and somewhat high-pitched. 'Have we met before?' He looked at me intently, his eyebrows bunched together the same way Gwen's would bunch when she asked a question. I remembered the bus station that first homegoing last fall; he must have seen me then.

'I don't think so.'

'Gwenny knows I'm coming.' He looked at his watch. 'I'm on time.'

We didn't know what to say to each other after that, so we just sat there in silence. It was awful; I wished I had stayed hidden in our room.

Luckily, after only a couple minutes, I heard singing. It was the Be Here Butterflies, coming up the stairs. Marigold came in first, belting out song and snapping her fingers. Amy was followed by Rawlene, and then Gwen, all swaying and snapping and singing. Amy's father followed stiffly, like the cap on a bottle of fizz. There was no Nicole.

Mr Perle stared at Gwen as she moved through the lobby with the BHBs. I couldn't tell if she noticed him, but she acted like she didn't. She stayed in line and boogied down the hall, out of sight.

Mr Perle had a frantic look in his eyes. 'What was that?'

'Just some of the girls,' I said, 'plus Gwen. I'll go get her.'

I found them in Amy's room. They were sitting cross-legged on the beds, watching Marigold *get down* in the middle of the room. *Iddy biddy* Marigold could really hoof it; her patent leather Mary Jane's squeaked on the wooden floor. I sat next to Gwen, and whispered, 'Your Dad's here.'

'I know,' she said. 'I *saw* him.'

'You can't just leave him out there.'

'He's left me enough times.'

'I don't think he's married anymore.'

She looked at me. 'No shit?'

'Well, he isn't wearing that wedding ring, and she isn't here.'

Gwen nodded, her curls bouncing around her face. She pursed her poppy lips. Standing, she announced, 'Yo, my old man's here, see ya 'round.' She winked at me, and headed for the lobby. That was the last I saw of her for a while. I stayed with the Butterflies for a few minutes, and then Ted came in to tell me Dad had arrived.

Walking down the hallway seemed like forever. It had suddenly occurred to me he might have brought Lisa. If she was with him, I decided, I would turn around and shut myself in my room. I would walk away.

But Dad was alone, sitting in Mr Perle's old spot on the couch, looking gaunt and sad. My apprehension melted.

When he saw me, he smiled, and a gentleness glowed in his eyes. I kissed him on the cheek.

'How's my girl?'

'You're not even late,' I said, and hugged him.

'I made a point to be on time.'

I got my jacket, and we walked down toward the school building. Clusters of kids and parents and siblings dotted the campus. I was surprised to see Peter Prentice, standing by the main gate, wearing a three-piece suit under his pea coat. His grey cap sat on his head like a pancake, and his cold red hands dangled at his sides. A black limousine glided to a stop near him, and an elegant, silver-haired woman stepped out and kissed his forehead. A tall man emerged from the other side and waved. Peter got into the limo and they drove off.

'Kid's got money,' Dad said.

I couldn't believe it. The one time I had asked Peter about his background, all he had told me was that he was adopted as an afterthought to a late marriage. He never mentioned he was rich, or explained how he'd landed at a place like Grove. Maybe he had gotten kicked out of all the expensive prep schools for being too weird, and some therapist steered him here, to the Grove Loony Bin. I stood there with Dad, watching the limo snake away. Why hadn't Peter just asked his folks to fund the dome? If my parents had had that kind of money, I wouldn't have wasted a minute.

And then Dad said, seemingly out of the blue, though I expect this is what had been on his mind as we stood in silence at the foot of the hill:

'Well, the divorce came through.'

His hands were pushed deep into his pockets and his face was serious. I didn't know what to say. What *could* I say? Thanks for ruining my life?

We walked in silence to the school building.

'Are you going to marry *her*?' I said.

His face tensed. 'Lisa and I are no longer together.' After

a pause, he added softly, 'This whole thing has been a big mistake.'

It was like my heart was a sponge sopped in conflicting feelings and someone squeezed it. *Pain, happiness, regret, hope* all flooded me. I was happy Dad and Lisa had broken up. But poor Dad; he seemed so strangely diminished. My father, my strong daddy, why was he being so crazy? Leaving Mom, leaving Lisa, and regretting it all now. Acting so compulsively. Dad, who was supposed to be the one most in control, was the least.

'Who left who?' I asked.

He said, 'We left each other,' and shrugged.

It didn't take much to figure out that she had dumped him.

His face lit up, and he said, 'Can you keep a secret?'

'Me?' I smiled. Secret-keeping was never my forte. 'Sure!'

He laughed. 'I'm going to ask Mom to marry me again. What do you think?'

Mom and Dad, remarried? I said, 'I think she'll make a great wife and a nifty step-mother!'

'Just don't get your hopes up, Kate. She may say no.'

I could hardly picture Mom refusing Dad — but there was Jerry now. Even so, how could Jerry possibly stand up to all those years with Dad? In my mind, he couldn't. Dad would be the ultimate hero of this nightmare-turning-dream. I was thrilled!

'Dad,' I said impulsively, 'I want to show you something.'

I took his hand and led him through the Smoking Circle to the hill overlooking the science field. The unfinished dome sat firmly on frozen ground, around which islands of snow looked like clouds. Senior the snowboy had partially melted and then frozen into a formless lump with a piece of wilted newspaper on top.

'What's this?' he asked.

'It's going to be a geodesic dome. I'm building it with a couple other kids.'

He looked at it in silence. I couldn't tell if he was moved or baffled.

I said, 'I just thought I'd show you.'

'I'm glad you did.' He put his arm over my shoulders and hugged me. It felt so good to be with Dad. He was my father again, not Lisa's lover. I was sure he would bounce back to normal, that soon he would be too busy and happy and full of life to be on time.

After a tour of the rest of campus, we went back up to the dorms. Junior, who had told me his mother was coming, was sitting in the Upper Girls lobby in a little brown suit and a red bow tie. Marigold was next to him on the couch, holding his hand. I blew Junior a kiss and he hid his face, giggling, in the crook of Marigold's neck. She didn't seem to mind.

Mr Perle was sitting in a chair with Gwen leaning against its arm. Dad sat down on the other side of Marigold. She gaped at him. Maybe he looked like an alien to her, so tall and grey with his longish hair waving over his ears. *Super honky.*

I never really expected Flower Booker to show up, but she did. She entered like royalty: tall, proud and beautiful. She was light-skinned and with her almond eyes, long nose and ruby-tinted lips, she looked like an Egyptian queen. She wore black suede thigh-high boots, and a long black wool cape over a red minidress. Junior broke into a huge smile, like a little man whose love had just breezed in. When Flower bent down to kiss him, her eyelids shone with silver glitter. Dad and Mr Perle stared. Gwen and I rolled our eyes at each other, and Flower winked at us with one of her sparkling lids. She didn't so much as glance at the men. She just lifted Junior, set him down on the floor, and led him out of the lobby.

Mr Perle turned red all the way up to his receding hairline. Dad crossed his legs, clasped his hands over his lap, and looked at his knees. Gwen and I started to giggle. And this, of course, was the scene into which Mom arrived.

She was followed closely by Jerry. They were both

energetic, smiling, happy. Dad's attention was rivetted to them. I had never told him about Mom and Jerry, and I guess no one else had either, because it seemed to come as a real surprise.

Dad stood. 'Hello, Molly,' he said. He nodded coolly at Jerry, who nodded back, then retreated across the room.

Mom's eyes traveled from Dad's blushing face to his groin, where a lump stood out beneath his brown pants. 'For God's sake, Max,' she said. Her mouth tightened into a thin line across her lower face, accentuating her wrinkles, aging her instantly. Looking right at him, she pulled off her red leather glove. She was wearing an engagement ring: a fiery opal surrounded by tiny diamonds.

Dad stared at the ring, and I could see the spirit fade from his eyes, the color drain, his pupils contract to tiny black pinpricks. He was shocked, disappointed, pained; he had the stunned look of someone who has just been blasted with the truth.

'I should be going,' he said softly. 'I didn't realize it was so late.'

'We're a little early,' Mom said.

Dad sighed. I was distinctly aware of the 'we' in her statement, and it must have sounded even louder, starker, to him. He got his coat from the arm of the couch and exited like an actor in a bit part no one would ever remember. Except me.

# FIFTEEN

A big pink card from Dad arrived in the mail the day before Valentine's Day: a ship sailing into the horizon of a frilly heart. There were bows and curly-cues everywhere, and three naked cherubs pointed little arrows at the ship. Dad had folded a separate note inside the card. He explained that he would be moving into a studio apartment, and gave me his new address. He also noted in a P.S. that I would always be his daughter. That threw me; I had never expected otherwise. Did he really think Jerry could replace him? Just because Mom was remarrying didn't mean my parentage was up for grabs. It couldn't be. I knew that, and I was sure Mom and Jerry knew that. Why was Dad feeling so uncertain? To reassure him, I cut a big heart out of red construction paper, and in fancy script wrote: HAPPY VALENTINE'S DAY Dad, Love YOUR Daughter Kate. I mailed it right away.

Patrick sent a card, too. His arrived in the morning mail on Valentine's Day, and I got it during breakfast. It came in a small red envelope with no return address. That was risky, I thought, because if for some reason I hadn't received it, he never would have known. Yet he had been thoughtful enough to plan for the card to arrive right on time, and I read a lot of meaning into that: his mind was clear; he loved me; he would be back at Grove soon. But when I saw the card, my heart dropped: Snoopy slept on top of his dog house with his girlfriend, the little yellow bird, hovering over him with a tiny red heart dangling from her beak. Inside, the card said Happy Valentine's Day beneath which Patrick had scrawled Patrick Nevins. It was just a packaged greeting as if from a long-forgotten acquaintance. I tried to hide the card from Gwen, who was sitting next to me, but she pried it away. She glanced at it, grimaced, and handed it back.

'I told you so,' she said.

My anger boiled: at Patrick for distancing me, at Gwen for judging Patrick, at Dad for questioning my daughterhood. How could the most important relationships become so tenuous? Why couldn't Patrick hold on to me as I was holding on to him? Why couldn't Dad have more faith? Why couldn't Gwen keep her comments to herself?

Silvera stood up to make announcements, but before speaking he paced in front of the fireplace behind his table. That meant he was about to say something to us, deliver one of his prophetic messages. I was dying to leave now, to dart before the man could spin a web of words around me. I hated his gummy, gooey, goopy speeches. Mr Know It All, Mr Tell Us How It Is, Mr Butt-In. I wished he would just leave us to grow up our own way, in peace; let us have our families, cling to memories, nurture hopes. But no, not Silvera, our dark prince of reality, hard and cold and forbidding. This time, his cynical message with which to start the day was:

'Tamara and I will be in my office today, listening to love songs and discussing the destructiveness of their false promise. Anyone is welcome to join us when you're not in classes or activities. Happy Valentine's Day, folks.'

Out in the Smoking Circle, there was talk of America's popular culture. I stood outside the throng and watched the other kids: they were like a nest of worker bees, Silvera's soldiers, echoing the queen's buzz. Silvera would do away with all vestiges of human connection, of love, if he had his way. He was wrong to want that. And he was wrong to influence us. In his godless scheme of things, I would not be one of the disciples he sent into the world to transform social philosophy. My heart and mind were repulsed by his rejection of the power of love. To obliterate even the most banal expression of love would be social suicide. The man was a killer. In all his preaching of love and sex theory, he had never even mentioned personal experience. Maybe he didn't have any? Maybe *he* was the virgin queen, the angel of destruction, the man in the black negligée!

I dragged on a cigarette and held the smoke in my lungs. It was freezing out and the smoke warmed me a little inside. I cleared a place to sit on the snow-covered log, and watched Gwen and John across the Smoking Circle. They stood close together, talking, their breath forming a cloud between them. They looked so much alike: both skinny with straight blond hair to their shoulders. Nearly a foot taller, John looked down at her, smiling, nodding his head. Was he finally responding? Was the only soil in which their undeveloped attraction could thrive one of the fat man's lovelessness? The great Grove doctrine: all in nothingness, each alone.

Gwen and John kept glancing at me. I pretended not to notice and lit another cigarette. When people started filing into the school building, Gwen waved at me to come along. But I just sat there. It was so cold. I wanted one more cigarette.

'Why aren't you in class?' It was Jimmy, on his way up to the dorms. What, I wondered, had he lost in the translation of Grove's principles to his own life? For one, he had lost Louise. She had left Grove the night of the school meeting, branded with a big scarlet A that Jimmy didn't seem to question. But how did he feel inside? Or did he? Since then, he had become one of Silvera's best generals, aloofly enforcing the rules. Didn't he see that if the man had chosen to handle Louise's error in agreeing to 'help' Eddie (which she never even did, in the end) as a misjudgement and not immorality, they could still be getting married in the spring? Silvera might have been more diplomatic, if he had understood the value of Jimmy's and Louise's relationship. They had loved each other. Silvera's rigid method destroyed it in one blunt stroke.

'I'm on my way!' I stood up as if I were about to move on. But when he was out of sight, I sat back down. I just couldn't bear the thought of going in to class. Inside me was a burning, an aching, a cry to leave, to scream, to tell the man exactly what I thought. That's what I would do, I decided. Fuck the rules, fuck the schedule, fuck being a good girl. He had said to go talk to him about love — and I would.

I climbed the stairs to Silvera's office on the second floor of the school building, and knocked. No one answered, so I pushed open the door. He and Tamara were listening to love songs, as promised. Or, love songs played in the background; there was no way to tell if they were really listening.

'I've been expecting you,' Silvera said. 'Come in.'

I didn't move from the doorway. 'Why were you expecting me?'

'No reason,' he said. 'Have a seat.'

I sat in one of the chairs in front of the round coffee table. Silvera leaned back with his hands folded over his fat stomach. His hair was greasy and his forehead looked tense. Tamara took a long drag on a cigarette and seemed to drift off with the song. I had a feeling she was in love with him. He probably knew it, and thrilled at the irony.

Silvera suddenly rocked forward. 'Don't you love this song?' he said.

Tamara nodded dreamily.

I couldn't restrain myself. I said, 'Do you know what a hypocrite you are?'

'I happen to like this song. Why am I a hypocrite?'

'You said these songs are sick. You said you were going to analyze these songs today. You're sick, if you want to know the truth.'

Silvera laughed. I wanted to hit him. I pictured the back of my hand striking his obese face, forcing his eyes away from me. I gripped the arms of the chair.

'They *are* sick,' Silvera said, leaning back again. Sweat gathered on his forehead and he wiped it off with a red bandana.

'Why are you so fat?' I asked impulsively.

His eyes flashed: hot, angry, black. 'Look, little girl, you parade around here like some kind of princess, but you're crazier than most of them. Why am I fat? I'm dealing with my problems. You deal with yours.'

What did he know about my problems? What did anyone know? 'I am,' I said.

'No, no, you're not. Why are you sitting here right now? Why did you come to see me? You want to talk about love songs? Huh? You want to talk about Patrick? He loves you so much, where is he now? Let's talk about love songs, little girl.' He grabbed an album cover from the floor and thrust it into my hands. 'Read the lyrics. Go on, read them. You've had that pumped into your brain since you were born. It's your responsibility to clean it out.'

'My responsibility?'

He flared his nostrils, nodded his head rapidly like machine gun fire, stroked his grizzly beard.

'I don't want to talk about love songs.'

'Then why are you here?'

I should have known that whatever I said would be twisted around, that talking to him would make me feel worse. 'I just wanted to tell you that I don't agree with you.'

He shrugged. 'So? Who expected you to? You're another kind of addict.'

'Excuse me?' But I knew what he was saying: that I was addicted to love, to possibility, to hope.

'You don't know anything about it,' he said.

'I'm not a virgin.'

He laughed. 'You have the most virginal mind I've ever encountered.' His nostrils flared, he was revving up. 'Having sex doesn't constitute experience.'

'Then what does?'

He tapped his skull. 'Use it.'

'Does *not* having sex constitute wisdom?'

He stared at me, livid. I had hit the nail on the head, *his* nail, his secret.

'You didn't come here to talk to us,' he said in a tight, low voice.

'You didn't exactly want anyone to really talk to you, either.'

'Emily Dickinson,' he said.

'What?'

'The great poetess of love. She pickled kittens in her spare time.'

'I would never pickle a kitten!'

'A sick mind,' he said, not listening to me at all, 'pent up in dreams.'

I stood. 'You're the kitten pickler.'

I think Tamara wanted to laugh, but she didn't. Silvera was too angry. I left quickly through the open door. If I had had my wits about me, I would have slammed it shut, just the way he really wanted it.

# SIXTEEN

All it took was a word to Gwen — 'I think the man's a virgin' — for the rumor to spread. It moved through campus as a sourceless bit of information, which some people believed and some didn't. But it caused a real sensation for a few days and I was satisfied. I hurt him by discrediting him just a little, and to my great surprise, it gave him pause. He actually called me to his office and delivered a simple apology for being rough on Valentine's Day. I accepted, and we entered a state of diplomatic grace.

In the meantime, the dome grew toward completion. Between Peter, Gwen, me, and Junior as our helpful elf, the work went quickly. By the beginning of March, the essential structure was finished. It looked like the skeleton of a moon that had thrust itself into the earth. It was a good time for us; we had become a team, sharing a common purpose. The dome. Nothing could keep us away from it. Except, of course, a glitch in the Grove machine.

As with all intrusions, it happened suddenly. It was after classes, on a windy afternoon. Peter, Junior and I were at the dome, just getting started, when Gwen came skidding down the muddy hill.

'There's a stealing meeting in Upper Girls tonight!' she called.

'What for?' I asked.

'I'm not supposed to tell,' she said, but Gwen could not hold back a secret. She whispered: 'Nicole says someone stole two bucks.'

'It could go on forever,' I said.

'This will interrupt production,' Peter said.

'I'll be here,' Junior said. 'Don't worry about nothin'.'

But stealing meetings *were* something to worry about. They had been known to go on for five days and nights, with only a few hours of sleep when wakefulness became unbearable, with only the snack food already in the girls' rooms and whatever the boys might send up. Smoking was allowed in the lobby during long meetings; it eased the hunger and helped keep you awake. All the furniture would be removed from the lobby once it was determined that the money had not been lost or misplaced, but had definitely been stolen by someone sitting in that very room. You couldn't even read, or talk, or doodle. Silvera's theory was that discomfort hastened truth.

All afternoon, I thought: *I haven't stolen anything, I'm innocent. Why should I sit through one of those tedious meetings?* I guess I was feeling some power from having humbled the man, if only just a little. I thought I had a choice. One of the great untested Grove theories was that you did not have to stay at a meeting if you didn't want to, though you would risk expulsion. I decided I would be the first to test it. I would not go. But I wouldn't run away, either. I would show up at the beginning of the meeting, explain my position, and leave.

All the girls were gathered in the Upper Girls lobby. When things quieted down, I got up and made my announcement.

'I'm not staying at this meeting,' I said. There was a general derisive groan from the mob. 'But I decided it was only fair to at least tell you why.'

'You realize that everyone has to be present at a dorm

meeting for it to continue?' Pam said in her stern, mannish tone.

'I know.'

'If you leave, you're automatically expelled from school.'

'I'm aware of that.'

'And if you leave this meeting and the meeting can't go on, you'll be leaving everyone here to live in an atmosphere of distrust.'

I could feel a scream building inside me like a spring. No. I sighed, and the spring tightened. *NO, NO.* 'I didn't take anything from anyone,' I said. 'If we all really trust each other, then you should trust me when I say that. I'm not going to sit through a meeting when I know I didn't take anything.'

'The rule is there has to be a consensus to determine that,' Pam said.

'I know the rule. I'm taking my option not to be here.'

'You can leave if you want to,' Pam said. 'But you're being selfish.'

*No.*

'I didn't have to come here to tell you people why I'm not staying,' I said. 'But I thought you should hear it from the horse's mouth. I'm not asking for an opinion, and I'm *not* going to stay. I didn't take anything and I'm not sitting here indefinitely until *she* realizes she left the goddamned two dollars at home!' I pointed at Nicole, and everyone looked. She was nervously running her fingers along her tightly cornrolled braids. Her normally bold, steady eyes were restless, darting around the room.

'Why don't you just stay until we determine if this is going to be a stealing meeting, Kate?' Dana said. She was short, with thick legs, wiry auburn hair and small hazel eyes. At dorm meetings, she really threw it around, playing arbitrator, prosecutor, defense, mom, sister, the works. She was a real Grover, always playing by the book for her own best advantage. There were rumors around school that she was having an affair with Ted.

'No.' I headed for the door. 'No.'

'It's your choice,' Pam said.

I was leaving, I was almost out, I was doing it. Then, when I lifted a hand to push open the door, Ted and Jimmy stepped in front of me to block my way. I thought of the dome — of finishing it — and of Patrick — of seeing him. *NO* moved me forward; I threw myself against them. My boots jabbed and my fists punched. Jimmy grabbed a handful of my hair and for a second I thought he was going to rip it out. The violence happened too fast for me to be surprised. Only afterwards did I realize that not only had I attacked two people, but one of them was my favorite teacher, Ted. But Ted was standing there with Jimmy, barring my way, denying my choice and my option. *They* were breaking the rule. I drew my boot back one more time, and looking straight into his eyes, thrust it into Ted's shin. He tried to smile but I could tell he was as shocked — by his authoritativeness and by my violence — as I was.

The room was silent. I may not have been forgiven, but I was understood. All the girls learned my lesson. No one had ever tried to leave a meeting before and now we all knew the truth: that what we'd thought was *shouldn't* and *won't*, was *can't*. Even Ted and Jimmy realized for the first time that the truth was *can't*.


Dana paced a small space of empty floor. 'The first thing we need to do,' she said, 'is decide whether or not the money was stolen, not lost or misplaced, but really stolen. So let's think back, Nicky. Where did you say you last saw the two dollars? Think.'

'In my top dresser drawer under my panties.'

'When did you last see it?'

'Yesterday afternoon before activities, when I came up to change.'

'Could the money have gotten mixed up with your underwear?'

'I already looked in the whole drawer. I checked everything.'

'Check again,' Pam ordered.

Nicole rose obediantly. She was a big girl, tall and muscular, with dark brown skin. A red plastic pic stuck out of her back pocket. Returning to the lobby, she reaffirmed what she had been saying all along: that the money was gone, missing.

'All right,' Dana resumed. 'If the money *was* stolen, then we know it had to have been some time yesterday between about three o'clock and this morning before breakfast, when Nicole noticed it was gone. Right? Did anyone have any visitors in here yesterday afternoon or night? Were any of the boys up here at all?'

'Maybe one of them snuck in when we were at dinner?' Alison said.

'And went straight for Nicole's underwear drawer?' Janice burst out. Janice, with her skinny legs, lanky brown hair parted in the middle, and the black leather jacket she never took off except to sleep. 'Nicole only wishes it was a boy in her underwear drawer looking for smells and not money!'

'Bitch!' Rawlene spat.

'I'm only kidding!'

'No, you're not.'

'Well, everyone knows you were a whore before you came here, Nicole — '

'White honky bitch!'

'Rawlene!' Ted said. 'Sit down!'

'I wasn't,' Nicole whispered, 'Never.'

'We're trying to find out what happened to the two dollars,' Dana said. 'That's all.'

'Maybe you spent it without thinking.' Lee Lee tried.

'I didn't spend it.'

A few of the girls fidgeted nervously. I sat completely still, staring through the window, watching tiny white stars shimmer against a black sky, feeling the night open like a pit of sleeplessness.

'What if we believed in ghosts?' Marissa said. Her pale skin was taut and shiny. 'What would we do then?'

'There's no such thing as ghosts,' Janice said.

'What I mean is, what if nobody took it, and it's just gone?'

'That isn't rational,' Pam said. 'It might be misplaced or forgotten or stolen, but it can't be just gone.' She pressed her lips together: two wrinkly slabs of flesh. Frustration. Tightening. The inevitable was coming: the call for a vote: a stealing consensus. That was the worst possible thing. A concensus was a lock, sometimes a rusted lock that wouldn't open with any key.

Dana watched Pam, and shook her head. Nicole stared guiltily into her hands. My heart dropped.

One by one, each girl gave the word, agreeing to continue the meeting. No one liked it, but according to Grove logic, it was inevitable. It was too late to turn back. The missing money was acknowledged, there were rules.

*Stealing. Stealing. Stealing.*

'Maybe I don't have to know,' Nicole said. 'Maybe the two dollars don't mean that much.' Her round face was tense, bunched like a prune. Something was worrying her more than the meeting.

Jimmy shook his head. 'It's too late to stop the meeting now.'

Within minutes, furniture was removed from the lobby. All that was left was the baby grand piano, and a room full of anxious girls in quest of a thief or the truth, whichever came first.

'Hey!' Amy shouted into the silence. Faces lifted. She stood up and opened her arms like one big mother of everyone. She sang: 'Silent night, holy night, all is calm . . . Hey, hey, heyeyey!' She swung her hips. In a rush of excitement, girls reached for cigarettes and blew every size smoke ring into the middle of the room. Rawlene jumped up and did three Ford Highways in a row. Everyone laughed and clapped. A cloud of smoke gathered in the center of the room.

Dana whistled loudly, curling her top lip. 'Okay, does anyone want to confess?'

Our giddy laughter stopped short. We had been cooped up for hours, sitting on the hard floor, waiting for an answer, hoping for a little sleep before morning. A few faces looked like they might produce tears, though none did. Others seemed to contain shouts. Others, accusation.

'Maybe we should do the x's?' Lee Lee said.

Doing the x's was always a last resort. When trust broke down, when there was no longer any real hope for a candid confession, everyone was given a chance to confess anonymously by dropping a slip of paper with an x on it into a box, or bucket, or tub. The x's made it easy to tell the truth, and easy to lie. Sometimes, someone innocent would leave her x behind just to end the meeting.

Pam shook her head. 'It's too soon for that. Let's give the person a chance to confront us in person.'

I thought about Marissa's ghost, the one Janice was so sure didn't exist. What if it did exist? What if ghosts were something other than what we assumed them to be? Maybe secrets were ghosts waiting to be revealed, like the thief. Maybe a ghost was watching us at that very moment — you could never tell. I squinted my eyes and saw it, our own personal ghost, in the cloud of smoke that was flattening into a smooth layer and rising toward the ceiling. I watched the smoke-ghost move above all of us, trying to escape us and our eager promise of absolute trust. When finally the layer of smoke reached the ceiling, it melted into the corners and fled in scalloped grey puffs down the walls.

I said, 'If it were me, I wouldn't feel comfortable confessing to any of you right now.'

'Was it you?' Pam asked. The revulsion in her eyes was so frightening that Loretta, the quietest girl in the dorm, recoiled into a cat-like ball beneath the piano. Her face was completely hidden; all that could be seen was her fluffy black hair encircled in her arms.

'Was Patrick here yesterday?' Pam asked.
'No,' I said. 'I haven't seen him in a long time.'
'How long?'
'Almost three months.'
'Why don't you try three weeks?'
'What are you talking about?'
'Wasn't Patrick here a few weeks ago?'
'No!'
'You knew he wasn't supposed to be here,' Pam said.
'He *wasn't* here.'
Pam shook her head. 'He was seen,' she said, 'coming out of this dorm.'
My heart pounded. Patrick, here? 'Well, if he *was* here, I didn't see him.' I looked around at the faces of my dormmates, and asked, 'Who saw him?'
'I did,' Jimmy said. 'At about four in the morning on a Tuesday night.'
Did he sneak in and watch me while I slept? While I dreamed of him — and *her*? Had he actually been there? If only I had opened my eyes. . .
Nicole moved tensely. 'I only want to find out who took the money,' she said — as if she knew I wasn't the one.
'I don't think Kate's relationship with Patrick is really the issue,' Laura said.
'But we can't trust Kate, can we?' Pam said. 'Kate isn't here with us. Kate's somewhere else.'
'So what?' I said.
'Did you go to the woods with Patrick that night?' she demanded.
'I did not even see him!'
'Oh, come on, Kate!'
Suzie Zuckerman bolted up from a slouched position and laughed nervously. 'I don't know but it sort of sounds like you want Kate to say she got high or had sex or something you know what I mean? I mean I don't know maybe I'm wrong but it sort of sounds that way to me. I don't know,' she said, waving a bloated hand in the air. She readjusted

her stiff black wig, and her back melted into its habitual curve.

'Why don't you just accuse me of taking the money?' I asked Pam.

'I thought you said you didn't take it.'

'Kate didn't take the money,' Gwen said. 'I was with her all day yesterday outside of classes.'

Janet raised her hand. Her thick blond hair was tied back in a pony tail and her brown eyes looked big and round and soft. 'Can I say something?' There was a chorus of 'Sure,' 'Go ahead,' 'Who's stopping you?' and her hand fell limply to her lap. 'I have an idea,' she said. 'Why don't we go around the room and everyone can say where they were between three o'clock yesterday and this morning?'

'Good idea,' Dana said. 'Let's go in a circle, starting with Nicole.'

'You all know what I did,' Nicole said. 'And Amy and Rawlene, they were with me the whole time.'

'Uh huh,' Rawlene said.

'It's the truth,' Amy confirmed.

Now came my turn. 'I was at the dome after classes, then dinner, then study hall, then I read on my bed until lights out.'

Gwen exhaled a rush of smoke, and said, 'Same.'

Alison smiled nervously. 'I got my period yesterday,' she said in a small voice. A rowdy cheer filled the room: we all knew how long she'd been waiting to join the ranks of puberty. Despite her enormous breasts, and even though she wasn't a virgin — thanks to Eddie — she had been just a little girl until now. 'Dana showed me what to do and Silvera was here and he thought I was sick and I didn't want to tell him why. He said me and Dana could stay up in the dorm for activities. Dana made me some tea and we went to dinner together but I wasn't hungry. After study hall I went to bed. I didn't feel too good.'

Suzie's back straightened. Her head perked up like her neck was a spring. 'Pam roomed me!'

'That's right,' Pam said officiously. 'Suzie was in her room after classes until dinner, and after study hall until bedtime.'

'Let's see,' Marissa started dreamily. 'Nathan walked me up, and he waited for me while I changed into my leotards. After dance, Nathan walked me up and waited while I changed for dinner, then he walked me down. After study hall, he walked me up and we sat on the fence. Then he walked me back and I went to bed.'

Dana delivered hers perfunctorily: 'I was with Alison until dinner. I came up to the dorm after dinner to monitor honors dorm study. Ted and I were in the lobby, talking, until lights out.'

'I was pretty depressed yesterday all day long,' Laura said. 'After classes, I went up to Silvera's office and we talked for a while. I really needed to get off campus, so he said I could take a walk to the mall if I promised to bring him back some ice cream — '

'He's supposed to be on a diet!' Amy shouted. 'He told me he'd throw me out on my ass if he caught me breakin' my diet! Hippo-crit! You're all my witnesses! If he gives me any hash over a chip or a bar, you're all my witnesses and we'll just tell him we know about his ice cream! Man might as well just paste it on his belly.'

'You're on!' said Janice. 'Baby, you is on!'

'Okay,' Pam said impatiently. 'Laura?'

'I got back just in time for dinner. I have honors dorm study now, so I came up here.' She sighed. 'Then I went to bed.'

Loretta raised her head from within her folded arms, and smiled. She seemed scared but that wasn't unusual. Loretta's great misfortune in life was that she had a lively imagination but no courage; there seemed to be a whole world in her head which she watched in helpless awe. 'I ate a muffin in my closet,' she said, and nestled her head back in her arms. Then, after a minute, 'I put on my soccer shorts. I went to the soccer field. I wore a dress to dinner. I put on jeans for study hall. I put on my nightgown because I wanted to go straight to bed. I was tired.'

'Me and Janice came up and changed,' Jane said. Like Janice, Jane talked tough and wore leather. 'Played soccer. Changed again. Ate dinner. Changed again. Went to study hall. Changed again. Made out with Larry on the fence for forty-five minutes exactly.' She winked and elbowed Janice, who smiled. 'Bed and sleep. The routine.'

'Same routine,' Janice echoed. 'Except for Larry.'

Pam prompted detail.

Janice sighed. 'Came up with Jane. Changed for soccer. Played a mean game. Showered and dressed for dinner. Didn't change for study hall last night. After dinner me and Ford Highway hung out at the canteen and talked about —'

'Cars!' came a chorus from the girls.

'I'm in love with Ford Highway!' Janice shouted. 'We went out to the woods and *did it*!'

Groans of disgust and amazement charged her onward.

Lowering her voice and arching her eyebrows, she said, 'He couldn't get it up, so I said —'

'Buick Skylark!' Amy shouted.

'Okay, next!' Pam yelled.

Janet sighed. 'After running, I came up, and Sandra had hurt herself, so I had to find some bandaids, and went over to the boys' dorm. Walter gave me a few bandaids, and I came back and gave them to Sandra. We were late getting dressed, and — you all heard Silvera.'

Janice said in a loud Silvera voice: 'Who the hell do you two prima donnas think you are? Dinner's at six!'

'After dinner, Sandra and I came back up and we did our homework together. Then we went over and picked up Gary, and the three of us went down to the canteen, and played pool until bedtime.'

Sandra was dressed all in black. Even her hair was black. She wore a black star tattooed on her wrist. When it came her turn, Jane noticed that her wrist was bandaged and asked her why.

Sandra very slowly raised her eyes to Jane's face. They were the darkest, slowest, saddest eyes in the world. 'I didn't want the tattoo anymore,' she explained. 'I tried to scrape it off with a razor. I don't know, I thought you could scrape it off. I didn't know it was so permanent.' She covered her bandaged wrist with her other hand. 'I had no homework study hall until activities were over. Then I came back up here and was just thinking, you know . . . I was thinking about how I didn't like my star anymore, and I thought I could cut if off. Then Janet came in and told me to stop. She was right, I guess. I mean, it wasn't really working. So I needed a bandaid. It's not so bad, it doesn't hurt much. I hope it's not infected.'

Ted said, 'It sounds like you want it to get infected. Taking a razor to your wrist . . . what were you really trying to do?'

Janet turned a startled face to Sandra, and held her hand. 'She just wanted the star off.'

Sandra stared at her black stockinged knee. She nervously pulled a snag, and a run zipped up her thigh.

'It's not true, Ted,' Sandra said in a quiet voice. 'I just don't like the star anymore. When I put it there, well, I just didn't think it was going to be permanent. It was stupid.'

'You put it there yourself?' Ted asked. 'How did you do it?'

'India ink and a needle.'

'Did you sterilize the needle first?'

She stared at her knee. 'I don't remember.'

We had all spoken now, and everyone appeared innocent of theft. But then, were one to confess, one would simply confess. Our glimmer of hope that someone might have said *I had soccer and showered and took Nicky's two dollars* was gone. We were all innocent, yet we were all guilty, too. Guilty until proven innocent. That's what the meeting was really all about.

As we sank into late-night-early-morning silence, fatigue engulfed us, and slowly we reclined into our own private thoughts. I think Pam would have reached into our heads if she could have, and turned off our minds. But she couldn't.

I escaped through an empty frame that hung on the wall. It was a picture frame but with no picture inside. I had put it there myself one day, and called it a 'picture of silence.'

Ted was my English teacher, and when we were reading *The Stranger* he said to us, 'Let's not just talk. Remember when we read *The Hobbit*, we spun the room with latex like a giant web? We didn't have to think about it. The web was our expression of the feeling we got from the story, the hobbits, their world. Now, what do you feel about *The Stranger*? How can we visually express the feeling we get from it?'

The classroom became completely still. I remembered finishing the book one night. I pulled my covers up to my chin and stared at the ceiling. Inside me was a great universe of empty space, no boundaries, just a sense of limitless space. That was where *The Stranger* had taken me — nowhere — and so I said, 'It was the most depressing book I've ever read in my life. I would never suggest it to anyone. It's full of meaninglessness.'

'Did you say "full" of meaninglessness?' Ted asked.

'I mean,' I tried to be clear, 'that the meaninglessness is vast, big, too big, with no limits at all. I know that existentialism is famous in France, but I don't like it, and I don't believe it's true.'

'How would you articulate that visually?' he asked.

My mind went blank. 'I wouldn't,' I said. 'I couldn't.'

'Off the top of your head, what would you do to the story, say, if you could do something to make it feel more comfortable to you? How would you change it? Quickly, without thinking.'

Since he was going to persist until I answered, I gave it a try. 'I'd limit the space the man lives in, because it's too big, and he can't see his own self, where his life is,' I said.

'Become an artist and show me that.'

'I can't.'

'Don't think. Just do it.'

That night after study hall, I sat in the lobby and thought about it. How to sketch emptiness? How to structure nothingness? How to sculpt air, mere space, into form, limits? At that moment, my view was of Laura smoking a cigarette on the couch. Behind her was the bare wall painted an ugly milky green. Then I saw it: a simple frame around nothing, kind of like the dome. The frame would define space and give the bare wall meaning by interposing on its square blank surface a miniature likeness of itself, an imbedded mirror reflection, a capacity for introspection. I went to my room and removed the picture and glass from an eight-by-ten-inch frame, found a hammer and nail, and hung the frame above the couch.

Later, when Ted walked in and saw it, I could tell by his face that he knew. I told him I called it a 'picture of silence' because space without limits frightened me and limits made me feel safe. That I could only endure silence when I felt safe.

Now I looked around the room at the dreamy faces of all my dormmates, and wondered if we were safe. Safe at that moment, in the meeting, and also safe in general in our lives. It was impossible to know. Certainly we couldn't walk around with frames around our necks. Somehow we had to frame our souls. I looked at Nicole's face. Her lids were halfway down her eyes, and she was staring at her hands which were folded on her lap. She didn't look very safe. In fact, she looked particularly unsafe, too frightened to even lift her gaze. There were thoughts inside that gaze, hard thoughts and troubles. Her eyes were too set, too solid to be full of dreams. I had a feeling there was something to understand in those eyes.

Then, out of the blue, Pam's voice snapped: 'Okay, that's it, it's time for the x's. Let's vote on it.'

It was *yes, yes, yes* down the line.
'Okay,' Dana said. 'I'll volunteer. Who else?'
No one spoke up, so I said, 'I'll do it.'
A bucket was placed in the bathroom connecting Jimmy's and Pam's rooms. Dana sat alone in Jimmy's room, and I sat alone in Pam's. Lee Lee ripped looseleaf paper into small squares. Half the slips of paper were left blank, and the others were marked with a single x. She distributed one blank slip and one x to each person, so everyone had two slips of paper. You had two chances to confess privately, to Dana or me, and one — the bucket — in complete anonymity.

'I want to remind all of you,' Pam said, 'not to drop your x in the bucket unless you took the money. Once we got two x's in the bucket. Both people were trying to end the meeting and it didn't get us anywhere.'

'Have the x's ever worked?' Marissa asked.
Silence. The answer was no.
One by one, starting with Ted, they filed through Jimmy's room, into the bathroom, through Pam's room, and back into the lobby. Some of them walked by me in complete silence, as if the occasion were too solemn to speak; others nodded or said hello.

Meanwhile, a commotion erupted in the lobby. The sounds were those of a good time, a party. Somebody was singing, and soon Amy's and Rawlene's voices rose in harmony above the din. I pictured Pam standing in the middle of it all, trying to stop it. She was clearly failing. Or maybe the festivities had her golden approval; maybe she was letting them have a good time just until the x's were over.

I didn't expect a confession. As far as I was concerned, doing the x's was just another system for passing time. And so I was surprised when, instead of automatically passing,

Janice sat next to me on Pam's bed. I leaned toward her, thinking *maybe* . . . but she shook her head.

'I didn't do it,' she whispered. 'It's better than that. Jane and me, we were dancing near the windows just now, and we saw his car.' She handed me a piece of white paper folded into quarters. 'Patrick's here,' she said, and winked. 'No one else knows.'

I held the note in my hand while the last few people filed through. When the last person stepped back into the lobby, I unfolded it and read.

> Dear Kate, I'm driving down to Florida. I had to leave Eddie's. Silvera won't let me back into school so my parents said they were going to put me in a rehab. I'm straight now, I swear. Will you come away with me? *Please*. I don't know when I'll be back North again, maybe not for a while. I know we'll be happy.
>
> I love you.
>
> I have to leave at sunrise, before someone sees me. I'll wait until then. Love Me. (Patrick)

My mind reeled. Leave with Patrick? I could, I really could if I wanted to. I'd never been to Florida. What did it look like there? What would we do? I had three dollars and some change in my room. How would I get out of the meeting? What if we ran out of gas? And then there was the dome: I had worked so hard, poured so much of my heart into it, that it had almost become my love for Patrick. The thought of leaving before it was finished confused me — I wanted to see it through, and I also wanted to go with Patrick. If Dana had had a confession, or if there was an x in the bucket, then I would be free to choose.

I heard Dana in the bathroom collecting the bucket and shoved the note into my pocket. She came into Pam's room and looked at me hopefully. I shook my head. She sighed. I followed her into the lobby. The party fizzled out quickly, and everyone sat. I went to the window and looked into the pitch black morning. I could see the reddish gleam of a car, but Patrick was nowhere in sight. I was numb as we went through the slips of paper in the bucket. If only there was an x, a single x . . .

'What now?' Gwen pleaded.

'Who did it?' Suzie shouted.

'It isn't going to work,' Jane said.

'Quiet!' Dana shouted. 'Quiet! It *is* going to work. Just think for a minute!' Her voice cracked, her eyes were teary.

Rawlene pounded her fist on the floor. 'I'm sick a'this! This is crazy!' She looked around the room with drawn, stubborn eyes. 'I think Laura took it! Why don't we get down to business?'

'I didn't take it,' Laura said softly.

'I don't think Laura took it,' Alison said. 'I think it was Jane and Janice!'

Janice's voice was torn between laughter and defense. 'What are you talking about?'

'You. You think you own the world. You act like you can do anything you want. You're always saying you think rules are made for breaking. Well, I wouldn't be surprised to find out it was you who took Nicole's two dollars.'

'You're wrong.'

'Maybe I am. It's just what I think.'

'Yeah, well.'

'Okay then, who took it, smart ass?' Alison said.

'Girls!' Pam shouted. 'This isn't getting us anywhere.'

Ted raised his hand. 'Pam? Maybe it is.'

'Okay, ladies, who wants to box?' Janice challenged the whole room. 'Say it. Just say it! You all think I'm just a piece of shit!'

'Janice doesn't steal,' Jane defended her. 'And don't anyone say I do, either, because I don't! You're all mixed up, thinking tough means bad. You're all throwing value judgments to the wind.'

'Sleep is escape,' Suzie said. Everyone turned to her. 'Sandra's asleep.'

Eyes fled to Sandra, who lay huddled in sleep at Janet's side.

'Let her sleep,' Janet pleaded. 'She hasn't been sleeping well lately. She's been exhausted.'

'We're all tired,' Pam said. 'Wake her up.'

Janet nudged Sandra, who drowsily raised her head and propped herself up on her elbows.

'Sleep is escape,' Suzie said.

'Sleep is sleep!' Janet said.

My heart raced. The only way I could end the meeting would be to confess myself, but then I'd have to stay up and talk with the dorm parents. That would be impossible. If I wanted to go with Patrick, I would have to be free to leave the dorm, even through a back window, if necessary. I couldn't tell how much time passed, standing at the window, thinking. It felt like forever. I still couldn't see Patrick outside, and I still couldn't decide, if the meeting did end, how or even if I would make my escape.

It was a quarter past five. Sandra was asleep again.

'Wake her up.' Pam ordered.

'Everyone's falling asleep,' Janet said, pointing. 'Look, Gwen's asleep, Loretta's asleep.'

'Wake them up! Sandra, Gwen, Loretta, stand up!'

'Stand?' came a vague murmur from the floor.

'From now on, anyone who falls asleep will stand. No more second chances. And no more cigarettes, for anyone.'

'Nicole,' Dana pleaded, 'think back.'

Nicole's head rested against the wall. She pulled her head up and gazed at our faces.

'Nicole, *think*.'

Her face was too still. Something was happening behind her glassy eyes.

'Nicole. . .'

Early orange light began to temper the darkness. Was the sun rising? I searched for Patrick.

'I don't know,' Nicole said.

Brisk, clean air filled the room. It was better without smoke, but harder without cigarettes. Without the grey haze, morning seemed to rush in faster. Seven girls were standing now, including me. But I stood because I wanted to; I was keeping watch on Patrick's car and on the horizon line beyond the woods.

Finally, I caught a glimpse of Patrick moving restlessly beneath a tree. *Patrick.* There he was, in the flesh, for real, waiting for me. I still didn't know if I'd really leave for Florida, but I had to have the choice. I couldn't let the meeting make the choice for me.

'There's one question nobody's asked,' I said. I couldn't hold back my own suspicion, a crazy knowledge that had begun to haunt me.

Exhausted eyes turned in my direction, all full of the same question: who would be accused next?

'Nicole,' I said, 'did those two dollars really exist?'

Her eyes flickered, and she muttered, 'Yes.' Then, suddenly, she squeezed her eyelids shut. Her body jolted forward and she almost fell over. Amy moved to catch her. Nicole's eyes snapped open. 'No,' she cried. '*No.*'

'What do you mean, Nicole?' Pam asked. 'What are you saying?'

'She's so tired,' Amy said.

'No. There weren't any two dollars,' Nicole said, and she wept.

Everyone woke up. Faces were more alert than when the meeting had started.

'Nicole took her own money,' Suzie said.

'There wasn't ever any two dollars,' Nicole cried. 'I just said there was. I wanted to be with you all. I couldn't stand to be alone.'

'Why?' Ted crouched down next to her and held her hand.

'My mother's got no money left. Silvera says I don't do well enough for a scholarship. They say I have to leave here. I don't want to go. I can't go back! Mom said she was coming to get me today. I thought if the meeting went on a few days, she'd leave without me. But it's not even morning yet. I'm sorry. But I'm so scared.' Her voice shook. 'I'm so *scared*.'

'Is there anything we can do to help?' Ted asked.

'I want to stay here.'

'Your mother has no money left at all?' Pam asked.

'She says she doesn't have any,' Nicole answered. 'She says she can't pay for me to stay here anymore.'

'Nicky,' Janet said, 'you don't have to be the way you were before. There are so many things you can do. Finish school. You don't have to drop out just because you're not here anymore. You can be anything you want. Don't worry.'

Nicole cried in helpless convulsions.

'You all don't know what it's like out there for us,' Rawlene said. 'People think the civil rights changed things, but . . . ' She shook her head.

'I know everyone thinks I'm hard or tough or something,' Janice said, 'but I know what you're talking about, Nicole. It's safe here. But if you've got to go, then tell yourself, say: Nicole, I'm gonna make it work. And do it. Do it for Nicole the lady.'

'I'm sorry,' Nicole said slowly. She looked into her lap, away from us, as if our faces would hurt her.

'Do we have a consensus?' Pam asked.

Tired assent came automatically. Girls filed past Nicole, kissing and touching her as they went off to bed. There was no anger even after what she had put us through. Each one of us understood, in our own way, how terrifying it was when your only support system was about to buckle out from under you. And anyway, we had achieved the purpose of the meeting, which was to get to the truth.

I stayed in the lobby, frozen by the window. I could see Patrick pacing nervously beneath the tree. He was beautiful. He looked so strong — but he wasn't strong. That he would consume my strength came as a sudden thought. I watched him rub the inside of his arm, and I knew what my decision had to be. When he needed more than I could give him, he'd be gone again, hooked, lost. Alone in Florida with a junkie I loved. I couldn't do it.

Gwen came up behind me and put her hand on my shoulder. 'Are you okay?'

'I'm fine.' I shoved Patrick's note deeper into my pocket.

'Everyone's going to bed,' she said.

'I'll go in a minute.'

'You sure you're okay?'

I nodded. I didn't want to turn around. I didn't want her to see my face.

'Okay. See you in the morning.' She laughed. 'I mean, see you later.'

Patrick hugged himself against the cold. He stared at the windows of Upper Girls. Did he see me? I couldn't bring myself to move away.

# SEVENTEEN

We beat our own deadline and finished the dome at the end of March. In the final stages, I dreamed of Patrick every night. It would always begin with him in Florida, with his black-haired, pale-skinned girl, and end with me in my bed at Grove. The Florida parts of the dream were in technicolor, full of lush palms and emerald skies. Patrick would be wearing bright Hawaiian shirts and white pants, and his girl would be all in black. Her pageboy haircut framed her face like a window. Her eyes were grey, colorless, like mirrors. She never smiled, but her face was always taut, blandly amused. They would be happy and light together under the sun, and his hair would blow back from his face with the breeze. Her hair never moved, it was like a helmet. They would hold hands and walk toward the water, or sit together in the back seat of a bright red convertible with no driver, or sit at a small round table at an outdoor café like movie stars. Then, inevitably, they would move toward me. Color would fade from the dream, and Patrick would enter my room alone. He moved on the silvery screen of nighttime shadows and moonlight. He would be naked, his body smooth and pale, and he would slip between my covers and fall asleep. I would roll over into his arms and it was always at that point, just as I began to feel his body against me, that I would wake up.

I don't know what my dreams had to do with the dome, but I began to believe they were somehow connected. It was as if my love for Patrick and the spirit of the dome came from the same place inside me. Building the dome was a journey to that place. It wasn't over yet; I hadn't quite reached where I was going.

The day after we finished the dome, I stopped by after classes to look at it. It had been raining a lot and the ground was muddy. The dome sat on the wet brown earth like a half-moon that had plummeted from the sky. I skidded down the hill and stood in front of it. I felt a profound reverence, as in a graveyard; but it was not a grievous feeling. There was a loneliness to the dome, and a rich sense of peacefulness, too.

The whole structure was covered with the plastic triangles, completely sealed off. We hadn't built a door because, as Peter said, the dome was an idea, not a place. It was a bubble, his dream. But as I stood there, I became aware of a shadow moving inside. Then, suddenly, a muted scream emanated from the dome. It was Peter. He was inside.

Two-thirds of the way around, I found that one of the triangles of plastic was missing. I stuck my head inside and there he was, standing in the middle of the dome, his face beet red. Some kind of rope dangled from his hand. I had a quick and frightening thought that it was a noose, that he had built the dome as a place in which to hang himself.

'Peter! What are you doing?'

He smiled. 'Kate, how good to see you! Won't you come in?'

I pointed to the rope. 'What's that?'

He held it up. The rope was built of circles, like a stack of infinity signs. 'Come in,' he said.

I crawled through the small opening. Inside it was hot and damp like a greenhouse.

'What are you doing in here?' I asked. 'What's that thing supposed to be?'

He held it up high. 'It's a soul catcher,' he said. 'I made it myself.'

I stared at it. A *soul catcher.* 'You mean, like a butterfly net, but for souls?'

'Precisely.'

'Where'd you get that idea?'

'From a book on primitive artifacts. I saw a picture of one. It's supposed to capture lost souls.'

'Why?'

He shrugged his slender shoulders. 'I suppose that's up to the person with the soul catcher. In my case, it's just an experiment. Whatever souls I catch will be contained within the dome. Watch.' He twirled it above his head like a lassoo, and when he had gained some momentum he began to spin around. The soul catcher swung into a blur with a sharp whistling sound.

After a minute he stopped. 'Here,' he panted. 'You try.'

I twirled and spun with the soul catcher, like a helicopter about to take off. The feeling was free and fast and easy, flying, spinning into euphoria. When my balance went, I stopped. Coughing and laughing, I tossed the soul catcher back to Peter. He took another turn, then I did, then he did, until dinner time.

On the way up to the dorms to change, Peter stopped to break a piece off the branch of a tree that was just beginning to form tiny green buds. He handed me the knobby brown stalk.

'But it hasn't bloomed yet,' I said.

'Don't worry,' he said, 'it will.'

I kept the stalk in a glass of water on my dresser for two weeks. Clusters of buds were slowly forming. Then, one morning, I woke up to a glorious mass of purple lilac blossoms, filling our room with scents of sugar and spice.

It was spring.

# EIGHTEEN

During spring vacation, I stayed with Mom and Ann. Jerry was there a lot, too. But during the days when they were all at work, I was on my own. I moped around a lot, conjuring up demons. I missed Patrick, I hated Grove. I could hardly remember why I hadn't gone to Florida. Mom, Ann and Jerry seemed convinced my condition was some kind of readjustment anxiety because of the divorce. But to me, it was a bona-fide broken heart. They tried to cheer me up with movies and jokes and elaborate meals. Nothing worked. Then, one morning, Ann made me an offer. She said I could work in her boutique for the rest of my vacation, in exchange for some new clothes. I accepted half-heartedly but with a feeling of relief.

It was my very first job. Watching the gate roll up on the storefront was like a curtain rising at the theater; beyond lay the excitement and mystery of new worlds. Ann unlocked the door, flipped a few switches and the dark store came alive. The first day, I smeared on some of her pink lip gloss and waited for customers. One by one, they came: women of all ages and sizes and temperaments. By evening, I was a real salesperson; I felt I could sell just about anything to anyone. We locked up at about seven-thirty. It had been a fun, exhausting day and I decided I would like a life of work.

'Maybe I'll hire you for the summer,' Ann said.
'No kidding?'
'You did good. Pick something out for yourself from the sale rack.'

It was only April, but the sale rack was already full of spring clothes Ann wanted to unload to make room for new summer arrivals. For me, everything was the height of fashion. I tried on five things, and chose a green short-sleeved dress with a scooped neck, tapered waist and flared skirt. The tag said *Fiesta* and that was how the dress felt: like a party at night on a beach, with salsa music and Japanese lanterns and true-love-kissing. I looked at myself in the dressing room mirror and felt a warm flood of pleasure at the young woman the dress brought out in me. Patrick loved me in green. I decided to wear the dress the next time I saw him.

As Ann and I walked home, I imagined us doing this every day, a team. Maybe, I thought, when I finished high school, I could take some time off before college and work for her. I could get my own apartment, have my own life.

Then, to crown the day, there was a postcard from Patrick waiting for me at the apartment. He wrote that Florida was hot, that he lay on a pearly beach and swam in emerald water, that he wished I could see all the tilting palms. He wrote that he missed me and was sorry I couldn't join him that night of the dorm meeting, but that he understood. He loved me, he wrote. He said he was looking for work and when he had saved enough money he would send me a bus ticket. He promised to write again soon. The card was so full of tiny scrawl, there was no room for him to include his address, if he had one. Maybe he was sleeping on a beach, in the lush warm air, under a palm. The thought charmed me.

Mom and Ann laughed at me for letting a postcard from a boy send my spirit soaring. Mom was sitting at the kitchen table, wearing a yellow sweatsuit and sneakers in which I was sure she did not intend to exercise, and Ann was in an apron making dinner.

'You don't understand,' I told them. 'You're jaded. Can't you remember what it was like to be in love?'

'Now and then it comes back to me,' Mom said. She wiggled her opal and diamond ring.

'It's different when you're young,' Ann said. But I saw her wink, and Mom's half-smile.

I daydreamed of the apartment I'd have in the city in a couple of years. It would be on the bottom floor of a brownstone, on a tree-lined block, and the big bedroom windows would overlook a garden of red tulips, sunny daffodils and cascading roses. The brass bed would tumble with down pillows, all lacy white, and Patrick and I would live in that bed together. We would be married, really married, right away. We would own a store like Ann's and run it together. In time, we would have a small family, and the store would sustain our simple life together, a good life, solid and forever.

My nightdreams transformed, too. I was the heroine now, the happy girl under the palms. I was dressed beautifully, in bright colors, and Patrick was strong and certain in his faith in our love. All threats had vanished. In one dream, Patrick and I danced at Mom's wedding. I knew in my mind that Jerry was the groom, yet when the groom turned around, it was Dad. The rabbi turned into Jerry and he married my parents. Another dream was of Junior in the dome, sitting underneath the soul catcher, which dangled from the highest point. But instead of being black, Junior was white, and he was my and Patrick's child. Flower Booker materialized in the dome and kissed the top of his head. As she hugged him, he melted into her, then she vanished too and all that was left was the soul catcher swaying in the empty dome.

The postmark on Patrick's card told me it had taken four days to reach me. Thinking he might have contacted his mother by now, I tried calling, but there was never an answer. I tried for days, but the phone would just ring and ring. I even took her number with me to *Smithereens*. There was a small office in the back, and every so often, when there were no customers, I would try again.

It was at about two o'clock on Thursday afternoon when, to my surprise, Mrs Nevins answered.

'Hi, it's Kate!' I said. There was silence at the other end. 'Hello?'

'Yes, hello.' She sounded tired.

'I was wondering if you've heard from Patrick yet. I thought maybe you had a phone number or address for him.'

Nothing, just more silence.

'Mrs Nevins?'

'We just got back from Florida.'

'I thought you were away. I've been calling. Did you see him? Where is he? Who's we?'

'I went with Patrick's father. Dear, I'm sorry.' She paused. 'Patrick . . . He died. He's here with us now. The funeral is tomorrow.'

In the background, I could hear the bell on the front door, and Ann's voice calling my name.

'What?' I said. My hand was shaking. My throat, when I spoke, felt numb. 'Hello?'

Mrs Nevins's voice sounded distant, like it was a million miles away. 'He overdosed, dear. In Florida. If you take the noon train tomorrow, we'll pick you up. Please come. He would have wanted it.'

Ann stuck her head through the door. 'Hey, blabbermouth, it's getting busy out here!'

I think I looked at Ann but I couldn't see her face. It was a woman's face, eyes beginning to question, staring. The only thing I was aware of was the smooth texture of a pad of paper under my hand. Then the room began to fade and my stomach felt violently nauseated.

'Who were you talking to?' Ann asked. 'What's wrong?'

I swallowed the vomit that lurched into my mouth. I couldn't speak.

It wasn't true.

'Are you all right? Kate? Kate!'

The room faded completely. I couldn't swallow it back. I tried to stand, but my legs felt rubbery. The last sensation was of a pair of strong hands gripping me under the arms.

The police had found him lying on a sidewalk in Miami when the sun rose. He had shot some bad heroin into his arm, and died.

I could still feel him as if he were alive, standing in front of me, holding me. Orange hair curling over his forehead. Pale round face, blue moonbeam eyes. His back firm and warm against my hand. His breath on my ear. Our legs twined together on our New Year's bed.

Mom tried to talk me out of going to the funeral, saying it would only make me feel worse. But I had to go, I had to see Patrick off. In my heart, though, I did not really believe he was gone. Dead. Each time the word came to mind, my emotions blanked. It didn't make any sense to me. How could someone you knew, someone you loved, someone on whom you pinned your dreams, be simply obliterated from life? It was impossible to me that I would never see Patrick again. Wasn't I going to see him now, preparing myself to visit his home and meet his parents for the first time? He would be there, waiting for me in his parents' house. I could not imagine that he would be unable to open his eyes and say hello, to kiss me.

I had planned to wear my new green dress the next time I saw him. I cut off the *Fiesta* tag and prepared to wear it now. I wanted to please him one last time by wearing something pretty, a dress of one of his favorite colors. I couldn't believe that we would never share our thoughts and feelings and bodies again. I could feel his hands on my breasts as I stepped into the dress. My nipples shivered and hardened. I felt so weak, I couldn't pull the zipper up. It was as if he were passing through my body, stealing some of my life, and I had no resistance. Every time I moved, nausea rose to my throat. I wanted to crawl back into Mom's bed, where I'd huddled, frozen, despairing, for a day and a night. I couldn't eat; the thought of food sickened me. I smoked cigarettes to suck back the nausea. I lit one now, and sat on the bed with the zipper spread open across my back. All of a sudden I felt cold.

When I got off the train, I saw a couple standing against the railing and knew they were Patrick's parents. The man had short blond hair and blue eyes, and the woman had red hair and pale skin. To me, they looked more like his children, similar bodies that resembled him, had been born of him. Patrick was the original, his colors and features were the ones I knew.
When his mother saw me, she stepped forward. 'You're Kate,' she said.
'I can't believe it.' It was all I could think to say.
We walked in silence to the parking lot and got into a blue Buick. It must have been Mrs Nevins' car because she drove. Mr Nevins sat beside her. I had to remind myself that they had been divorced for a long, long time. Now, the last shred of their union was dissolved. The death of an only child of divorced parents completes the reversal of love; whatever had once been between them no longer existed in anything but memory.
Mrs Nevins lived in the modest white split-level house where Patrick had grown up. He had described it to me, and I recognized it immediately as we pulled up. Peeling white paint, green window boxes sprouting red geraniums, a long straight walk leading up to the front door. Cars lined the street. The neighborhood was eerily quiet. Two small children played in a yard next door, but otherwise there was no sign of life. Just death. Everything felt so empty, so stark.
Visitors sat in the living room. So much black. So much silence. A bay window let in the bright sun, but no one sat where it was warm, everyone sat in the shadows. Against one wall was a large electric percolator, a stack of styrofoam cups and a pyramid of sugar-dusted donuts. My eyes traveled over the staring faces of the mourners, to the table, and

to the corner where another wall began. In the periphery of my vision I saw the long black coffin. I stared into the cool white corner for a minute, an hour, a thousand years.

Patrick was in that coffin.

The soft touch of Mrs Nevins' hand jolted my gaze to the right — to Patrick. Tears sprung into my eyes, and I looked at her. Her short red hair was curled tightly and she wore clip-on pearl earrings. Nothing, though, no makeup and no smile, adorned her face. It was roundish and pale and her eyes were dim, embedded in puffy folds. She leaned close to me and whispered, 'Go see him.'

I felt the mourners' eyes on me as I crossed the room to the coffin. They were looking at my green dress and trying to see my face. I felt their eyes stuck like glue all over my body as I leaned above the coffin. I felt trapped, I couldn't breathe; their eyes would not release me.

Patrick was dressed in a grey suit that made him somber and dignified in a way he had never been. I leaned closer, just a foot above his face. His closed eyelids were round and perfect like the dome. Tears rolled down my cheeks and dripped from my chin onto the severe shoulder of the ill-fitting suit. I'd never seen such a white, peaceful face. Such stillness. I leaned even closer, nearly in the coffin myself now. I felt his body on top of mine on the princess' bed, his breath on my neck, whispering, 'Kate,' and 'I love you,' and pushing himself further into me. I could feel the sharp pain between my legs as my heart contracted into a tight fist. I stopped breathing, just stared at him. Patrick, my husband, wake up. But he just lay there, frozen, aloof — dead — his body straight and his arms folded over his middle. Someone had parted his hair on the wrong side.

Just as I noticed a glimmer of gold on his pinky — our ring — a voice whispered, 'The hearse is here.' It was Mrs Nevins. She drew me away, and a man in a dark blue suit lowered the lid of the coffin.

We got back into the Buick and Mrs Nevins started the

engine. Mr Nevins turned around and smiled sadly, and I saw that he had his son's eyes.

The funeral procession moved slowly along the unfamiliar web of streets, through and beyond a small town, and onto a highway. I felt no sense of time as we drove. Eventually the line of cars, headlights shining into the bright sunlight, snaked into an exit. We were in another town now, but its small boxy houses and manicured lawns looked just like the Nevins' — until we reached the graveyard. Then we were in another world. The rolling expanse of lawn studded with grey tombstones was like nowhere I had ever been, though I had passed many graveyards before. I had never seen, *felt* beneath the surface before, understood what was buried there. Now I knew: a graveyard was full of love, it was an airtight treasure chest, never to be opened, locklessly shut tight forever.

We walked past tombstones until we reached a newly dug grave. When I saw it, my fist-tight heart expanded in a rush of blood. Patrick's final bed. I desperately wanted to lay there with him. A small group of people gathered around the grave. Some of the mourners shaded their eyes against the sun but I let it burn into mine.

A bald priest all in black stood at the head of the grave. After a moment of silent prayer, he spoke. I barely heard the eulogy, but certain phrases sliced through my numb brain. *Martyr. Tragedy. Symbol of today's youth. A lost generation.* The priest was wrong. I wanted to say something, but what? It would have been like trying to talk to Silvera: a waste of time. *We were not symbols, we were not toys.* It was the society of our parents, as much as our own reaction to it, that was casting us out. Patrick's death was an example of nothing but a series of mistakes.

The shining black coffin was lowered slowly into the ground. The grave was filled with soil. A breeze made my dress balloon upward and I forced it down with my hands. Mrs Nevins was crying into Patrick's father's chest. The funeral party dissembled as two men smoothed the grave with the backs of shovels. There was no tombstone; it had all happened too fast.

Later, I re-read Patrick's postcard. Beaches. Palm trees. A hot sun.

Jerry and Mom insisted on taking me out that night. They chose an expensive restaurant on the East River, with blue table cloths, long white candles and a wall of windows that let in too much night.

'It *is* a beautiful evening,' Mom said. She looked at Jerry and smiled sadly.

'Kate!' Jerry suddenly said. He indicated my wine glass with his chin. 'Make a toast.'

'There's nothing to toast.'

'I can think of something.' He lifted his glass. 'To my son.'

'You don't have a son,' I said. I didn't want him to try to cheer me up; he didn't understand.

'I did. I will always have a son, in my heart.'

'Jerry,' Mom said, her hand on his arm. 'Don't.'

'I want to tell her about him.'

'Not now.'

'I think this is the perfect time. To the memory of my son, David. David was fifteen when he took his life. I will always love him and never forget him. Please, toast David's memory with me now.' He lifted his glass again, and waited.

My eyes stopped focusing and Jerry's face became a blur. Patrick, I thought. Who was David? How had Jerry survived the death of his own son?

'And to Patrick,' he said, his glass still raised. 'To two good boys who didn't make it through. And to a wonderful woman who did. And to a beautiful girl who will. To life.'

Our glasses touched above the table with a tiny clink.

The next day I called Dad and invited myself over for dinner. Dinner was just an excuse; I couldn't eat, I just wanted to see him. I wanted him to know how much I loved him, *that I would always be his daughter.* I guess I needed to know he would always be my dad. He didn't question the lifeless tone of my voice when we spoke on the phone. Mom must have told him.

He was living across town in an old West Side brownstone, where he occupied a studio apartment on the third floor. I was surprised at how tiny it was. It seemed overfurnished with only a twin bed, a card-table and two chairs. There was a single window. The white walls looked greyish, as if they hadn't been painted in years. The wooden floor was dull and scratched. A bouquet of fresh yellow tulips was the only sign of life in the whole place. I suspected he'd bought them that day, for me.

'Nice place,' I said, but didn't mean it.

'Well, I'm comfortable here,' he said. 'I planned to buy something nicer eventually, but I'm thinking maybe I'll stay.'

'It's a nice place,' I said again, nodding, thinking of how lonely and sad it felt.

'You don't have to say anything, sweetheart. Have a seat at the table. I made chicken. You always liked baked chicken.'

He brought out a bottle of wine and two wine glasses that still had price stickers on the bottom. As he served plates of chicken, broccoli and rice, the phone rang.

'I won't answer it,' he said. 'I don't want to talk to anyone tonight. This is too special.' He lit a candle.

It relieved me that there was someone out there who wanted to reach him, that maybe he wasn't as alone as he appeared.

I tried to be talkative and lively, and I could tell he was making a big effort, too. But I just couldn't shake the feeling that my life had been buried with Patrick's. We had not even known each other a year, yet I felt we had been born together. Dad and I didn't mention Patrick at all that night. But as he put me into a cab, he kissed my forehead and told me, like a fact, that I would be all right. I sensed the depth of his own desperate feeling of loss and error, and instead of

**gliding right over me, his words sank into my heart.**

> *Everything will be all right.*
> *To the girl who will. . .*

# NINETEEN

By the time I got back to Grove, everybody knew. There was a sense around school that Patrick was some kind of hero who had fought valiantly and been struck down suddenly in a great battle. But that was as far from the truth as the priest's martyr interpretation. Patrick was no hero, and he was no martyr. He had needed some confidence to live his life, and found it in a potent chemical that killed him. He might have lived instead. It was that simple.

Everyone knew why Patrick had died — and when and how and where — but no one would say it. *Patrick's death was pointless.* No one, that is, except Gwen. She was the only one who treated it specifically, not like some generic tragedy. Even Silvera, who summoned me to his room, disclaimed what had happened. He said, 'We couldn't really help him here,' and shook his head. But I didn't need the fat man to tell me that Grove was not the answer to our problems.

I lay awake in bed all that night; my body was exhausted, but my mind wouldn't stop asking questions. Why did Patrick die? Was there meaning in his death, or just the arbitrary ending I felt inside? Were my feelings for him permanent, as I so deeply felt them to be, or would they dissolve in time? Where was he now? From whom would I derive my deepest love? To whom would I offer it?

Finally, at about five o'clock, I got out of bed. I put on my faded jeans, an old yellow sweatshirt, and my red ProKeds. I tried to be quiet, but the door hinges squeeled.

'What's going on?' Gwen said in her scratchy wake-up voice. She sat up and looked at me. Her eyes were open in tired slits, and her hair was molded in kinky bends from too much hair spray. 'Where are you going?'

'I'm just taking a walk.'

'Where to?'

'I don't know.'

'Hold your horses,' she said. 'I'm coming with you.'

'I'm not running away, I'm just going out.'

'Wait. You need me.'

I could have sprinted ahead and left her in the room, searching through her neat piles for something to wear, but I didn't. My desire to be alone was vague, undefined. I did need someone, and maybe I would let it be her. It didn't seem to matter much who it was. A voice, a body, someone next to me.

We crept out of the dorm together, into the damp early morning.

'Jesus F. Christ,' she said. 'It's cold.' She laced her arm through mine, pulling me close. 'That's better. Where to?'

'Do you have a cigarette?'

She pulled a pack out of her jacket pocket. 'I have a lighter somewhere,' she said, fumbling through her other pocket. She pulled out a handful of papers and handed them to me. 'Here it is.' It was a white Bic lighter with a red heart on either side. 'John gave it to me, isn't it cute?'

We hovered over the small flame and lit our cigarettes. Then she handed me the lighter. 'Keep it,' she said.

'But it's from John.'

'I'll buy another one. He'll never know.'

I put the lighter in my pocket. 'Let's go see the dome.'

'I knew that was where you were headed.'

'I didn't.'

'Yeah, but it's the only logical place.'
We walked down the path arm-in-arm.
'Do you ever think about your abortion?' I asked her.
'Sometimes. Why?'
'Does John know?'
She shrugged. 'Maybe.'
'Don't you think it'll make a difference? With John, I mean.'
She tugged me closer. 'You mean if we ever *do it*?'
'I guess.'
'I don't know.' She paused. 'Are you pregnant?'
'Sometimes I wish I were.'
'Hey, Patrick's gone, it wouldn't change things.'
'At least I'd have something.'
'Perfect. You'd be a teen mother of a dead junkie's kid. Face it, it wouldn't exactly be romantic.'
Tears came suddenly. 'You don't understand!' I shouted, pulling away from her.
'Hey, no one. . . Look, I'm sorry. I'm not trying to hurt you, I just want you to see it like it is.'
'I know he's gone.'
'Do you?'
'I love him, Gwen. That hasn't stopped. What am I supposed to do?'
She sighed. 'I don't know.'
We finished our cigarettes in the Smoking Circle. 'John says he liked me all along,' Gwen said. 'Hey Kate, what about Troy?'
'What about him?'
'John says he has the hots for you. I bet he'd dump that Janice if you said the word.'
'Gwen — '
'I'm thinking of your future.'
But in my heart, I didn't have one. I couldn't even think of another boy. All I wanted was to dive into the earth after Patrick.
We went to the science field and sat at the foot of the hill

looking at the dome. Wisps of pink and purple were weaving into the darkness: morning was coming. Gwen took out two more cigarettes and asked for the lighter. She lit both cigarettes at the same time, gave me one, and pocketed the Bic.

'Did you hear about Nicole?' she said.

'What?'

'She ran away from home. No one knows where she is. Probably hit the streets again. I feel bad for her.'

'Why couldn't Silvera just let her stay?'

'Money, I guess.'

Gwen stared at the dome. 'Did you see Peter?'

'No.'

'He said to tell you there was something in the dome. He's so fucking mysterious, he wouldn't tell me. I think I see something though. What is it?'

In the pale rising light, the dome assumed a milky transparency. I could just see the soul catcher dangling in the center, swaying very slightly. Its shadow rocked like a pendulum, slowly grazing the rounded inner walls.

'It's a soul catcher,' I said.

'What the — '

'A soul catcher. I can't explain.'

I understood. Patrick was in the dome, harnessed by the soul catcher. *A dream.* He had become a real part of Peter's mystical building block, and a post in the structure of my spirit. Leaving the soul catcher in the dome was a statement — not about the stark, sad fact of Patrick's heroin addiction, but about the value of the life it destroyed.

'Fuck it.' Gwen tossed her burning cigarette butt down the hill. It sizzled on the wet grass. 'It was just a simple question, but don't do me any favors.'

I sighed. 'It's supposed to capture lost souls.'

Gwen leaned her shoulder against mine. We watched the pale orange sun rise over the dome, which glowed faintly as light crept up the sky.

Morning: beginning locked tight with ending. Patrick was gone — there was nothing I could do.

We waited until all shades of darkness had been swallowed up. Then we started up the hill toward the dorm.